*Don't Leave Me*

# STIG SÆTERBAKKEN

# DON'T LEAVE ME

## A NOVEL

Translated by Seán Kinsella

**DALKEY ARCHIVE PRESS**

Orignially published in Norwegian as *Ikke forlat meg* in 2009

© CAPPELEN DAMM AS 2009
Translation copyright © 2016 Seán Kinsella

First edition, 2016
All rights reserved

Library of Congress Cataloging-in-Publication Data

Names: Sæterbakken, Stig, 1966-2012, author. | Kinsella, Seán (Translator)
    translator.
Title: Don't leave me / by Stig Sæterbakken ; translated by Seán Kinsella.
Other titles: Ikke forlat meg. English
Description: First edition. | Victoria, TX : Dalkey Archive Press, 2016.
Identifiers: LCCN 2015044152 | ISBN 9781564788474 (pbk. : acid-free paper)
Classification: LCC PT8951.29.A36 I4413 2016 | DDC 839.823/74--dc23
LC record available at http://lccn.loc.gov/2015044152

Partially funded by the Norwegian Ministry of Foreign Affairs,
and by a grant by the Illinois Arts Council, a state agency.

This translation has been published with the financial support of NORLA

www.dalkeyarchive.com
Victoria, TX / McLean, IL / London / Dublin

Dalkey Archive Press publications are, in part, made possible through the support of
the University of Houston-Victoria and its programs in creative writing, publishing,
and translation.

Printed on permanent/durable acid-free paper

# Contents

*If God wanted to wipe humans off the face of the earth, He would grant them knowledge of what awaited them.*

# Death in June

PICTURE IT. You're twenty-one years old and you know your life is over. Society is evil. Everybody is evil. If you had a nuclear bomb you wouldn't hesitate. Yet you're aware of the teeming street below. The hum of engines. Talk. The clacking of heels on the pavements. A clamor of impatient movement and life. Summer is here! For the very last time! Voices, footsteps, music, digging, drilling, banging, sirens, activity that attests to the plans and energy that abounds, all of it reaching you. But you're not a part of it. You have been, but not anymore. What formed the connection is gone. And what's left is worthless. Nothing is holding you back. It won't cost you anything to leave it.

She, on the other hand, is out there taking part in what's happening, more active than anyone in the circus of life that's taking place. Nothing is left to chance with her, everything fits together, all linked up in a single terrible movement, the grinding wheel that is the destruction of all reserve. Nothing is prevented, no one controls or restrains themselves, expression is everything, uninhibited, debauched living, wild indulgence, a never-ending series of excesses, capturing all those who are up for it, who are willing, who want to play the game, and mercilessly excluding all who do not.

The society of the living: those who gather every night to laugh scornfully at the faithful. You berate yourself constantly. You threw away your only chance. Happiness was here, now it's gone again. You're back where you started, where you were supposed to be the whole time. You exceeded the boundaries that were set and were brought back, back to where you belong. You did as you pleased, mixed with people from another world than your own, loved a girl a hundred times better than you, were

3

loved in return, like in a dream, the last and most agonizing of them, the one that plays such havoc with reality because it takes place seconds before you awake. You enjoyed life; that was your crime. You thought life was a game. You walked with your head held high. You thought that you'd mastered it. You told yourself that life was good. You let a feeling of happiness and perfection hold dominion over your heart and mind.

Your crime, which you must now atone for, was to confuse the dream with reality, to believe that this wonderful new world belonged to you, that it was all here to stay, that this was how it was going to be from now on. You believed that what had become yours in such a fantastic fashion would continue to be yours. You sneaked over to life on the sunny side, but were caught red-handed and put on the first bus home, back to the valley of the shadows.

Amalie's parents were right: you were just a civil servant disguised as a poet. You were one whose likes they'd seen before. You were the flaw in the picture, the one no one missed when he was gone.

Now the fairy tale is over. You're back. You're home again. In the mirror: the biggest idiot in the world. No, not an idiot, just a pretty ordinary boy, in a pretty ordinary place in the world, with a pretty ordinary future in front of him. An average person, a young man of his time, one who doesn't distinguish himself in any particular way, who's neither conspicuously stupid nor sensationally smart, one who has a reasonable chance of succeeding in the goals he sets himself, but no more. And who'll be obliged to be content with that. But who'll carry a memory for the rest of his life of that wonder, an image of the most beautiful one of all, as though he'd caught a glimpse through a doorway, into that world that would never be his, into a room bedecked for a party, into all that splendor that's not meant for someone like him.

You open the window. Kitchen smells seep out from all the buildings. People are eating. In apartments and at restaurants people have sat down at tables with full plates in front of them. Juicy pieces of meat, beef burgers and fried onions, potatoes, lettuce, sweet corn, chalk-white dollops of sour cream, overcooked vegetables, going down their throats in little lumps, blood flowing to their stomachs and their jaws working at full tilt, like a global time-out from the hustle and bustle. You wish they continued, that they never finished eating, remained seated for the rest of their lives, no one getting up and going out ever again, that the streets were empty, that cafés and nightclubs would have to close down, that no newspapers came out, all businesses went bankrupt, all trade ceased, that no ledgers needed balancing any longer, that no one met, no one touched each other, no one talked together or wrote to one another, everyone had to stay indoors from now on, no one fell in love anymore, no attraction would arise beyond that which was to be found, everything would exist in the shape it has, nothing else would happen, that the whole world went to bed, all activity, all desire for discovery, all packed together and put away like a box of broken toys.

But it never ends. Because this is the society of the living. Unstoppable. They move up and down the pavements. With your forehead pressed to the window you study them. People in a hurry and others dawdling. Some walking with short, determined steps, others sauntering. Several with mobile phones to their ears looking like they have toothaches. You see young women wearing red and black raincoats, some bareheaded, others with hats, some with headscarves. Men in their forties smoking while they walk. Middle-aged women with children or dogs waiting a long time before leaving the safety of the curb. Swaggering lads. Sulky kids. A man in a phone box, gesticulating like a lunatic in the cramped space, even though the person he's talking to can't see him. A couple on their way out of the supermarket with a shopping bag in each hand, the weight making them waddle like penguins. An old man trying to persuade his dog to defecate in a flowerbed so he won't have to bag the excrement. And you think about God, how you pictured him as a boy, the enormous foot that would appear one day and kick in the wall with the mountains and sky on it, causing it to fall down and reveal the real world, right there in front of you, seething and boiling, filled with flayed, screaming people. Why is there nobody down there who takes on the job of putting an end to it? Where have all the executioners, the killing machines, and the bloodthirsty sadists gone? Or drop three tons of napalm, that would do the trick. If they don't want to be fenced in and like wide-open spaces so much, then they're fucking welcome to them!

But you know: nothing can stop them. They follow their given course, every single one, as though through the holes and along the passages of an anthill. Even those who hang back or just plod along are following a fixed course. None of them give in. They all keep things ticking over. Riddled with worries and anxieties but refusing to express them as long as they're among other people. They adapt to the multitude, fall in line with the larger scheme of things, the incessant stream, by neatly keeping quiet about anything that could slow it. They don't want to be a hindrance. They want to be part of the flow. They show no signs of weakness, any of them, not out there, on the busy thoroughfare, not before they get home and close the door behind them. But once there, surrounded by one or two or three of the people closest to them, they can be themselves again, as if by an unpleasant transformation, where everything that was taut and vigilant, becomes careless, slack, bloated and crumpled. They go from falsity to authenticity, and it's not a pretty sight. Even the attractive ones, the relatively good-looking ones, turn ugly as sin as they drop the promenade versions of themselves, at the moment they release their stranglehold on their public facade. What happens is this: they cease being the person they want to be and slump into the person they are. From having played their part to perfection, out there in the open, suddenly, within the safety of their own four walls, they become bitter, aggrieved, self-pitying, sad characters again, in that game which is no longer a game and is therefore interminably tragic, tragic without any extenuating circumstances, tragic without being simultaneously beautiful.

You turn in the hope of finding her behind you, of her having been there the whole time, of only having imagined she was gone. But she's not there. You've no idea where she is. You've no clue who she's with. She could be anywhere. She could be standing with her arms around someone for all you know. Someone she knows or has just met. She's probably embracing someone tightly at this very moment. Looking into his eyes, refusing to let go. Smiling at him with all her heart. Then she turns serious. Then she smiles again. Then serious again. They look so good together, everything fits, their heights, their builds, the length of their arms, every single inch of their bodies, they're inseparable, as if crushed together by a giant fist.

You want to disappear, run away, sink into the earth and forget everything you know and never hear about The Mortal Wound in the World Up Above: love. The word alone makes you sick, your stomach swells, a slimy intestine trying to find a way up through your throat. That's what love feels like. But that's the last time. Soon you and it will both be history.

You walk out onto the balcony. Its black bars reminiscent of a little prison. The evening is clear, the dying sunlight making a narrow band of flat clouds resemble a row of little orange baguettes. You stand hoping for a catastrophe, for something terrible to occur, something that affects everybody, that everything will disappear, a hole will open up and an earthquake will take everything down with it into the abyss. But nothing happens, ordinary life just continues on, all the activity, all of society, every aspect of everyday existence is stronger than ever, nothing can budge it, everything is set to go on as before, brutal and ruthless, without you. You're surrounded by it, but you're not a part of it. You're the one little hole in all of it. The only place the ends don't meet. One tiny void in the entire thing.

You remain standing on the balcony, on show for the entire

world to see. But no one notices you. You're all alone. You're going to die soon, but no one sees you, no one knows about you. You stand, raised high above the noise below, as if in the shovel of a digger right up until there's no difference between what's inside you and what's outside, right up until the noise and din of the others has seeped in and permeated you. There are only two worlds: the inner and the outer. Only two habitats for the living: either on the outside or on the inside. And confusion reigns in both. A person is a membrane between two forms of chaos.

And you picture her, out there somewhere, strutting unabashedly along to allow herself to be swallowed up by the city once more, among glittering shop windows, flashing café signs and seedy facades, into the nooks and crannies of discos and nightclubs, in among all the roars of laughter, all the moaning and all the ringing telephones, unrelenting men who'll all try to chat her up, touch her, breathe in her ear, run their hands up and down her back, kiss her hurriedly, go down on her if she gives them a chance, take her from behind in the toilet of the nightclub if allowed, black shadows swaying behind frosted glass, fantastic silhouettes, a terrible mixture of desire, exertion, and illusion seething in the swarm of people coming and going, mixing and mating with each other, separating and disappearing, at the same time as another identical swarm heaves itself into the mix before it too perishes and the whole thing, with her in the middle of it, with her as its natural center, will pull further and further away from you, the city will grow unfamiliar to you, the more she gains control of it the less of it you'll recognize, it will leave with her on board, the world will be lost on the horizon like a gigantic cruise ship while you are left standing alone in the harbor, the biggest fool of all: the idiot, the wretch, the monogamist, the gullible half-wit.

The Most Beautiful One

You have tried calling her, but it's Kim who answers the phone every time. You know that she's there, but never picks up, and you dare not ask for her. You never see her. You look for her everywhere. But it's as though she's vanished. You see all the others. But not her. Every time you meet Kim it's just as uncomfortable, he greets you just as awkwardly. Every time he's on his own. Like he's keeping her hidden, like she's locked up in his apartment, lying there all day in his bed with her legs spread waiting for him. A mutual acquaintance buys you a few beers one night, out of pure pity it seems, and tells you about a party he had been to, at Kim's place, where Amalie danced naked on the table. You learn from some girls you both went to school with that she'd suddenly got back in touch, that she'd called them and suggested they meet up, and that since then they've begun to socialize again. And they tell you how nice it is, how full of life Amalie seems, how wild they've been, the parties she's taken them along to, and how exciting they are, the new people she's introduced them to.

"Anyway, what about you, Aksel, how are things with you?"

She's dancing now, Amalie. She's floating. Finally she's got rid of you, finally she's free. Finally living the life she was supposed to. Finally coming into her own just as her parents wished her to. Finally she is where they want her. Finally her days have become how they were intended from the beginning: a wild party, a sensual dance, a horny, anarchic celebration of the splendor of existence.

You feel pressure in the pit of your stomach, the pressure from a void. Something's been removed. And you know you'll never find anything to put in there, not anything that fits. A doctor prescribes you pills that make your hands sweaty and give you eight hours of dreamless sleep each night, when you wake up in the morning it's like you need to familiarize yourself with everything all over again. You don't recognize yourself. You don't remember what you used to think about, recall what your brain used to busy itself with, cannot identify any of the thoughts knocking around in your head. You've forgotten what you did when you were a person. Everything has been swept away. What you liked and what you didn't like, you've no idea. Distinctions elude you. Hamburgers and shampoo smell the same. Your dick feels shriveled up, nothing can stir it, the thought of nudity doesn't arouse you; it's as though you have relinquished everything you had of gender. Nothing weighs upon you, no worries, no pangs of conscience, no uncertainty or doubt, nothing, you're as light as a hole.

You think about how you ought to take your own life, but you aren't up to it, haven't got the energy, the mere thought of everything that would have to be arranged exhausts you. You sign up for university prelims instead, sit at the back row taking careful notes of everything the lecturers say, without taking in one word of what is being said. But other times you lie in bed all day, unable to get up, wrapping the duvet around you, curling up in a ball and staying like that, bent around your own body, dreaming that the world doesn't consist of anything more than you and this duvet, this hollow, this warm, glowing cavity which protects you.

*Amalie . . . My heart is bleeding . . . And you do not know it . . . You do not even know where I am . . . You have no idea where I went to . . . You are in a different place seeing completely different things . . . I am here and see only you . . .*

There's no point in thinking about anything else. She lurks within no matter what. She stands at the end of every single path. She was the most beautiful thing life had to offer, by some fluke you were singled out to possess her, and by some malicious deceit you were lured into losing her. She was your driving force, whose departure left a dark core, the sole focal point, around which everything revolves. During the lectures, in the halls of the faculty building, in the white world of the canteen, on the crowded campus: Everything is her, everything is A. You see her gaze in the eyes of every girl who passes. You turn around at the behest of ghosts. Your heart begins to pound at the sound of the telephone ringing. You have a sinking feeling every time someone addresses you by your name. Yellow coats, no matter how seldom they are to be seen, make your head swim. All while you try to concentrate, all while you try to find your bearings in a world without her. You're utterly flummoxed. You can stand holding an object marveling over how it hasn't fallen from your hand ages ago. You can reply to questions and are amazed that others take what you say seriously, that it makes sense to them, that they're capable of being satisfied by what you say. You're astounded by the ease with which your fellow students socialize, their laid-back style, you begin to get the feeling you're the only one who's just started this autumn, that the others have already been there three or four years.

Kathrine, one of the girls from a study group you let yourself get talked into, buttonholes you and asks if you are doing anything special. Astonished by the question, you don't have the presence of mind to say yes. She becomes the first person to set foot in the wreckage of you and Amalie. You look around your dorm room. It's as though one can still see that someone's left, taking half of the stuff that was in there with them. And you think: The only thing there's room for here is to go to bed together. Yet desire is slow in coming. A full erection is out of the question. But you manage to attain a sort of semi-rigid state, just enough to accomplish intercourse. Only afterwards do you have the time to hold one another and explore each other's bodies. Everything about hers is so unfamiliar. Plump and firm, like that of a seal. The nails of her little toes are the size of pinheads. Her pubic hair almost see-through, gathered in a narrow curl up the middle. The skin difficult to run your hand across, as if the hairs have a braking effect. And when you run your hand down along her back you give a start: At the bottom, just above the cleft of her buttocks, where there should have been a moist little nest of downy hair, there's something hard and angular. You pull your hand away, twist loose from her embrace, sit up and swing your legs over the edge of the bed with your back to her, you hear her stir behind you, hear her voice, asking if something is wrong, but you haven't the energy to turn around, to say anything, to talk to her, just wish she would get dressed and go, disappear, never come back.

Just a brief "hi" when you pass in the corridor the next day. Followed by several more days where you don't exchange a word. You can't imagine a body more repulsive than hers. Then one day, during a break, she comes over and asks if the two of you can't hook up again soon. You say that you'd like that. When the last lecture is over you meet on the steps outside, you walk past the hospital grounds while talking about the lecturer, who you agree is awful, both of you having struggled to stay awake. Inside the dorm room the two of you stand in silence, she is just as much out of it as you are. She places her hand on your shoulder and smiles. A muscle at the corner of your mouth contracts weakly when you try, for the first time in four months, to do the same. Then she slips out of her clothes, lies down on her back in the bed and puts a pillow over her face. This time your dick sticks out from between your legs like a foreign object, freed from the sorrow of your body, so hard you almost come as the fair-haired pubic mound fits around it. She leaves the pillow there the entire time. She wants you to be spared seeing her. You hear her moaning behind it while you make love. Afterwards you lie there beside each other for a while, before she stands up and gets dressed. You don't say anything, can hardly wait to get her out of the place.

A few days pass, you sense her gaze upon you now and then, from the benches behind you in the lecture hall, or from one of the far tables in the cafeteria. Then, eventually, on the third or fourth day, she ventures over to you again. You continue to meet like this, with a gap of four or five days. You seem to be in harmony: The time you need to shake off the feeling of disgust coincides with the time she needs to work up the courage to approach you. The very act itself assumes a pattern, her on her back in the bed with her face behind the pillow, you, silent, on top of her. One time you tear away the pillow, you want to look at her, want her to look at you, want to have all of her, but she just turns her face away and lies with her head off to the side and eyes closed until you're finished with her.

But you do it for Amalie, it's for her sake you force yourself through with it. In order to show her that you're well able to tackle each day on your own, that there are other people to love, other people to fuck, that you're not dependent on having her around in order to enjoy what the world has to offer. Everything you do, you do for her, so that she'll notice it and bestow meaning upon it. You can feel his eyes in the back of your neck, no matter where you are, the private eye she's hired to trail you and report back to her, on every word you say, everything you do. And you can picture her, taking delivery of the detective's daily reports, a nervous expression on her face, terrified of receiving confirmation that you're doing all right, that you're managing, that you didn't need her after all, in order to live.

You meet her one last time. She calls you one day and says: "Hi, it's me," with an ease that sends a shiver down your spine. You have a few things belonging to her, some books and records, which she'd like to get back, would it be okay if she came by one day to collect them? Her chipper voice scares you out of your wits. Wasn't it the way you remembered it after all then, what the two of you had together? Was it something quite different, something fleeting, incidental, temporary, something one needed a week or two to recover from? Another experience to take with you? A small diversion along the path of life? A case of puppy love, never meant to last?

It's the beginning of April, the light harsh and cold in the mornings, car wheels crunch, raising dust from the streets as you walk to meet her. Because you know well which things are hers and which are yours, her records seem to glow with distinct colors in among yours. As do the books, you can see with a passing glance what had been hers, what had been yours. Why? Is it because they were never meant to belong to you both?

You were firmly against her first suggestion, of her coming to you. As if the student dorm, where you hadn't changed anything since she took her stuff and left, would carry an all too obvious message about how poorly you're managing without her, how bad things are with you, how indolent and inept you are, now that you don't have her? Or was it the sight of her, among everything you shared, that you feared, that seeing her there would mean losing her once again? Watching her walk out the door and leaving you once again? Being left there alone once again?

The handles of the shopping bags are worn thin when you reach the café, and you just about manage to carry the load safely in. She's not there when you arrive. You order a coffee and sit down at a table right at the back. You look up. There's a mirror in the ceiling. You see a round face on a flattened body. On the floor, leaning against the chair you're sitting in, the white bags with the logo of a cheap supermarket chain, in them the last of Amalie's belongings in your possession. You think: When she gets these bags, the last ties are cut. Then nothing is holding us together.

The bell above the door tinkles. You draw a breath without meaning to. You turn, relieved when you see that it's not her. At the very same moment she catches sight of you. A smile passes swiftly across her lips. She comes over to the table, says "hi" and sits down.

The transformation is astounding. Her hair is cut short and dyed red. One ear—she never wore jewelry!—is studded with small, shiny pearls. Another stud sticks out of the side of her nose. There's a pentagram hanging on a leather band around her neck. Her lipstick is crimson, her blouse is bright orange. And on top she's wearing an old biker jacket (whose?) which is way too big for her, the bulging shoulders full of white blemishes resembling dry, chapped skin.

"Hi," you say, smiling. What will you do? How will you act? Will you pretend that things are good? Let her know you're happy to see her? Or will you let it show, the hell that you're going through? How unbearable it felt when you saw her and realized that it was actually her? How loathsome you think she is, with her gaudy makeover (as if she has gone over every millimeter of herself, as if that was the point, that not even the smallest speck would remain unaltered from the time you lived together)?

And you realize: This is what she wants to show you. *The new Amalie.* Maybe that's why she called and asked to get her things back, you think, not because she needed them, or missed them, but because she wanted to show you how changed she was, what a complete transformation of personality she's undergone, how totally and utterly she has rid herself of whom she was when she was together with you? How wonderfully revitalized she feels, now that she's free from the prison you built for her?

She lights a cigarette, takes a long drag and blows out a sharp puff of smoke, practiced, self-assured, elegant, worldly, with the air of a movie star, cold and aloof. The matchbox she lays on the table bears the name of an awful nightclub, a paradise for married men on the prowl.

The conversation dries up, she seems keen to be on her way. She's the one doing most of the talking, you're responding. You try to think of something to say, something to pique her interest, or surprise her, or arouse her curiosity, cause her to regret having left you, to revive some of what once was, to plant a seed of doubt in her mind as to whether leaving you was the right thing to do. But you can't think of anything, you're too weak, too groggy to think up something to say, to even think at all. All you're filled with is despair, and you had decided beforehand to do all you could to keep that hidden from her. You sit there, polite and attentive—like a stranger—and listen, reply as coolly and calmly as possible to everything she asks about, remark, with a look of interest on what she tells you, which for the most part is comprised of odious trivialities from her odious new life.

Amalie glances at the bags.

"Will I manage to carry all that, do you think?"

And you offer to give her a hand with them, wherever she's going.

"If you could help me carry them across to the tram?" she says, picking up one of the bags herself, walking over and holding the door open for you.

Out on the street you follow close on her heels, like a servant. It's not far to walk to the stop, where you wait until the tram comes and help her on with everything. You want to say something to her, something which, just for a moment, could prompt a glimpse of what was, coax a smile, like the one you're privy to, the one only you are privy to, hear her say your name, one last time. But then the doors slam and the tram prepares to move, and you have to run up to the driver, who's irritated and gives you a telling-off. And when you're back on the pavement, craning your neck to look for her as the tram, with a plaintive cry, begins to move, you can't catch sight of her, she's not there, she's already gone, disappeared, vanished like a ghost and the doors close behind you.

You arrive home, lie down on the sofa and fall straight asleep, only to wake up a few hours later, just as suddenly, completely at a loss as to where you are. You stare into space. It's dark, the streetlights are on, it's quiet everywhere, night. You go over to the fridge, needing to lean so as not to lose your balance, take out a carton of juice and gulp down what's left. You stand there a while, your mouth numb from the strong taste, a belch bringing up a surge of sweet acid, at the same time as you're struck by a chilling feeling, as though something terrible has happened, as though a tragic accident has taken place. You feel a weight in your hand, as light as a small stick, for just a brief moment, then it disappears again, like an anxiety attack that couldn't find a place to get hold, because everything inside you is flat and featureless. Then you realize it must have been something you dreamt. You can barely remember it. Something about a loud bang, deafening you, and Amalie screaming. Or rather, you see that she's screaming, but can't hear anything, just see the open mouth with the red edges, that ugly crew cut, that horrible row of pearls in her ear, that disfigured nose. You look at her face, which is completely distorted in fear, and you decide to follow the hideous features with the knife you're holding in your hand, make the grimace permanent. Then it's not Amalie anymore, but Kim. He's screaming at you too. You stick something in his mouth. And suddenly it's as though a new mouth opens in his face which swallows the old one. A gaping black hole takes his place. You turn to look for Amalie. But she's gone. You look for her everywhere, but can't find her anyplace.

In the darkness, beside the fridge, you remain standing for a long time, incapable of doing anything, trying to call the image of Amalie to mind. But now it's as though you can't recall either of them, neither the radiant figure who once set your heart alight nor the close-cropped vampire who arose from the grave to desecrate your memory of what was.

# Eyeball

YOU PICTURE IT, how she lets herself into the apartment and immediately starts undressing, even before she knows where he is, the man she's there to see. Discarding her clothes as she walks across the floor, as though she'd been out in the rain and got soaked through, her panties lying like a black puddle at the door to the bedroom. He's seated on the bed waiting. A shiver passes through her as she catches sight of him. They don't say a word, just look at one another, gravely. A gasp that sounds like a cry escapes her when he touches her. She lies down beside him. He takes hold of her shoulders. She slides underneath him. He pushes her legs apart, but fails to enter her on the first attempt. She guides him with her hands, eases him in. And they gaze at one another the whole time, gaze with the most awful, earnest look in their eyes.

Or is it just a friend she's visiting?

You've followed her across the city, from when she left home around eleven, yellow coat and purple boots, sheer tights visible between them and the hem of her coat, the frill of the short, black skirt showing. With an unabashed strut she sets off up the street, in the gray light, like in a French film, crunching along the winter grit on the pavement, her handbag on a strap over her shoulder, slapping, effortlessly, as though everything on her and around her partakes of her impatience. Heading toward what's long awaited. Quick steps. Clacking heels. Hair bobbing up and down. Her head turning this way and that, so wound up she can't help but take notice of everything around her, dazed and thrilled by all the details along the way. It's all so very clear to you. Room for everything living within her as she walked. She was receptiveness personified. Aware of everything. Except for the person following her, fifty meters behind, the one in the crowd, the one person who escaped her greedy attention, the one defect in her complete picture of this teeming spring day, the one who slipped behind a parked truck just as he realized she'd reached her destination and watched as she pressed one of the buttons and almost right away, without needing to speak into the intercom to announce who it was, was buzzed into the building.

You stand outside waiting. The apartment building towers above you like a thirty-thousand-ton colossus at dock, massive and unyielding, a terrible edifice filled with little rooms to hide in, as if made for dubious goings-on. It reminds you of a gigantic dresser, with drawers full of all sorts of secrets. And you can picture her, lying like a little figure in one of the drawers, lying there hardly moving while he busies himself with her, how she lets him twist and turn her into all the positions he wants her in, how she lies looking up at him imploringly, how she gives herself wholly to him and to what they have together, what they have alone, what no power in the world can take from them, what no power in the world can stop them from wanting.

Or is it just a friend she's visiting?

By the time she comes out it's started raining, you don't notice it until you see her turn up the collar of her coat. Slightly bent forward, she walks slower now than when she came, content, in no hurry, feeling lovely and relaxed no doubt, a numb sensation, happy in both body and mind, one would have to assume, as she clutches the collars of her coat together at her neck with one hand, making it look like she's holding an invisible umbrella.

And you renew the pursuit, like a movie played backwards, along the same roads, through the same side streets, the same park, across the same busy junctions. And with the recurrence comes certainty: the two of you are heading for perdition.

There's nothing to give her away when the two of you eat. Not the slightest sign to reveal what she's been doing earlier in the day, what she's engaged in, in his, the stranger's, arms. There's nothing about her now that bears witness to the pleasure that's only a few hours old. Not one trace of her transmuted self. She brings the fork to her mouth just as she would during any meal. Her appetite is an insult, an insult to you sitting there hardly able to swallow a morsel.

She's wearing the black cardigan, the zip-up one. Was that what she was wearing when they met? She's changed from the skirt into pants, obviously, that would have given her away, if she'd turned up at dinner with that on. You've searched through the laundry basket, without finding it. Not in her wardrobe either. So where is it? What's she done with it? Was it torn during the act? Or so covered in stains that she had to throw it out? Or did he break the zip when he tore it off her? Or did they even wait to get out of their clothes? Was that how it was? That she just went over and leaned up against the tacky wallpaper with her legs apart, ready for that first hard fuck that she'd been fantasizing so vividly about the whole way, from the time she left home until she was finally standing there in the room with him?

Or was it just a friend she was visiting?

Desire's most perfect fulfilment: doing it without a caress.

The newspaper lies on the table in front of her, open on the funnies page. There's a cloud sprouting out of the mouth of a man with a mask over his eyes, inside the cloud an exclamation mark. The opposite page is covered with cinema listings. Her gaze wanders down over the titles and times in tiny type. You pass her the salad bowl and at the same time ask if she'd like some more to drink. She doesn't reply, pays no attention to you, merely munches away while she lifts little tangles of green, red, and white onto her plate where it grows into a little heap, her gaze still lost in the damned cinema listings: what the hell is she doing, there must be a hundred movies there, is she planning on seeing every fucking one?

When she's finished eating, she puts down the fork, stretches her arms in the air and yawns loudly (exhausted from her earlier exertions!). Her jaw makes a series of slight, sharp noises, like the crackling of a fire. "Ahh," she sighs, smiling, apologetically, but in a frivolous way (worn out from this morning's gymnastics, woozy, sore and stiff, absolutely pulverized, as if somehow bliss itself had given her a good seeing to!). She asks if you want to go out and have a cigarette. Why the strained, unnatural tone of voice? Because she's taking great pains to behave normally, seem unaffected, appear reliable, dispassionate, absentminded, distracted? And in so doing gives herself away, that tad too eager that she is in her attempt to appear stolid. The only thing on her mind is the next meeting. Because she's nowhere now, she's right between two couplings with him. Couplings which don't dull, which only grow in excitement, which only make it even more unbearable to hang around at home waiting for the next time, the next meeting, which in turn makes them desperate to meet again, one more time after that, and then one more time after that again.

You're a combatant. You're standing facing the sofa with your winter boots on. You've been standing there for a long time. The sun has just gone down, a flock of migrating birds pepper the pink sky like small black seeds. You stand quite still looking at Amalie. She's sitting on the sofa in front of you crying. Her eyes are gleaming with fear. Your voice is hoarse from all the yelling, globules of spit shoot from your mouth as you scream once more at her that she's a whore, that you're going to kill her, that you're going to kill everyone who's fucked her. Finally your voice breaks and starts to rasp like an untuned radio. You look around for something to take hold of. First you overturn a lamp, it blacks out with a crackle as the light bulb smashes. Then you throw a chair at the wall. Then kick a table. A glass, two bottles and a vase explode on the floor. There's a sound of heavy footfall from the room above. You unhook the pictures from the wall and trample them to pieces, one by one. You push over the bookcase, the books slipping out heavily and landing in serrated rows across one another. Voices, then the sound of heavy banging on the door, followed by shouting, someone tries the handle. A stool hits the mirror, which remains intact for a moment, before vanishing in a cascade of tiny pieces. And you circle her the whole time as though it were a dance you'd rehearsed, you kick out at everything in your way, but at no point do you touch her, not once are you near her, as if that's the entire purpose, the challenge you've set yourself to overcome, to smash everything in the room to pieces while at the same time leave her without so much as a scratch. She screams every time something shatters, the rest of the time she cries. You're a combatant and she's your prisoner, under the protection of the Geneva Convention.

She moves out the next day, first to Marianne's place, and then after a little while the two of them find a bigger apartment. You know she's using her friend as a shield, using her to hide behind, making it, with her help, as difficult as possible for you to get hold of her, to phone her, get her alone. Like it's a strategy on her part, because she knows it will keep you in check, that as long as she keeps you in proximity of Marianne it will prevent any more of your outbursts. Nothing is ever clarified. She never ends it. Never declares the relationship dissolved. Just lets it pass, like rain you shelter from and wait to ease up. When you ask her, she's evasive, says the two of you can "be friends for a while, then we'll see." *Then we'll see* . . . the nonchalant way she expresses herself is like a piece of ice cast on the fire burning within you. But you'll go along with anything, you'll put up with whatever, just as long as contact is maintained, just as long as the tiniest hope remains, that the time will come when you'll find your way back to one another. Sick with yearning you'll swallow anything, no matter how degrading. Yes, even in the deepest humiliation, even in the worst shit there's hope to be found: the pain inflicted upon you and the suffering it gives rise to is the first step on the road to winning back your beloved. It's a test! You're being subjected to a test. Your stamina is to be gauged, your willingness to make sacrifices approved prior to the next step on the ladder of love, the one leading back up to heaven.

You fetch the red and black notebook and write:
*Darling Amalie . . .*
*Before I wake from this dream . . .*
*Will you put your arms around me once more . . .*
*Will you be with me one last time . . .*
*Be with me and hold me, like you did when you saved me . . .*
*Like you did when you raised me up from the filthy toilet of my*
*misery . . .*
*Raised me up and held me so I would not be flushed down and*
*disappear . . .*
*Took me by the hand and led me out of that stinking basement . . .*
*Showed me the world as a bright, happy place to be.*
*Do you promise?*
*Do you promise to stay with me and put your arms around me?*
*Do you promise to stay until I wake up?*
*Until you dissolve and disappear and everything becomes as it was,*
*as it always has been, as it*
*Always was meant to be?*

Christmas is approaching and you travel home together, she goes
back to her parents, and you to yours. Your mother asks about
Amalie but you just shrug. A few days before Christmas Eve she
calls, tells you there's a crowd of them going out and says "it
would be nice" if you came along. Her words tumble around
in your head after she's replaced the receiver, rapidly assuming a
false, mocking tone, then a hopeful, seductive tone, and before
long, one of genuine warmth and longing.

You force yourself to turn up half an hour later than arranged, so as not to seem too eager. They're all sitting there, around one of the tables at the back, beyond the dance floor. You get a shock when you discover Kim is next to Amalie. And for a moment it appeared to you as though he had his arm around her and pulled it away when he caught sight of you. Amalie smiles, waves you over to the table, but doesn't get to her feet: *she greets you like one of her friends, one of the gang, like anybody at all.* You find a chair and they make space for you. Some of Kim's friends are there, as well as some old classmates of you and Amalie. Three people are seated between you and her. People are talking in pairs. Amalie is chatting with Kim and the guy sitting on her other side. You make an effort to show some interest in what's being said, struggle to think of something to add, bringing your glass to your mouth constantly so as to disguise how often you actually drop out of the conversation. And you notice how the others look at you when you say something, as though they're astonished you're actually there at all, and seeing as you are, that you're capable of talking, that you still retain the power of speech, that you're sitting up straight in a chair and aren't lying on the floor sobbing.

Not once does Amalie look in your direction. She pays no more attention to you than she does to any of the others. *You have the same standing as them.* And she's seated too far away for you to address her, not without it attracting attention. You feel as though you're being squeezed from both sides. You feel as though you're stuck fast in the crush around the table. And you drink even more, to keep your hands occupied, to keep your nerves steady, to endure having to sit there in the throng, in this confusion that now exists for her, but no longer for you.

Only when you're standing in the toilet having a piss do you notice how drunk you are: you have to lean against the cold pipes to avoid falling over. On your way back you stop in the big archway onto the dance floor. Through the swaying crowd you see Amalie and Kim. Amalie has placed one leg over his.

She's turned into him, wriggling tighter into his embrace. She laughs. You see her white teeth, you see that beautiful smile of hers, and you think you can hear her laughter above the music. You remain standing in the archway. Now she's craning her neck toward his chin. You realize what she wants. She wants to kiss. She wants Kim to kiss her. Kim sits there grinning. Then he glances around—looking for you?—before moving his free hand down to her crotch. And you see her jut her groin forward to meet his greedy hand. Now she laughs even harder, stretching out her neck and pouting at him, trying to stick on tight. And then she catches sight of you, and instead of giving a start, terrified that you've caught her in the act, she does nothing to hide what she's doing, on the contrary, she merely remains in his grasp, at the same time as she holds your gaze, staring right at you, brazenly, laughing once again, her teeth glistening, as if there was nothing she could have enjoyed more than sitting like that with another man, unrestrained and uninhibited, knowing that you're watching.

You stumble out into the night, leaving the place behind. It's snowing. You run. You fall, get back to your feet, and fall again. You throw up. And you suddenly find yourself in front of the house where Zombie lives. You hold your finger on the doorbell, long strings of vomit and drivel hanging from your mouth, until the door is suddenly pulled open and you tumble over into the hall. You gabble away, half-propped, half-carried, words being flung around in an attempt to explain why you've come. A sickly smell hits you, it all wells up inside, like a new bout of nausea: all the things that have taken place here, the sad identification with a revolting fantasy version of the world the two of you were still too young to enjoy.

You're back. Back where you belong. In the place you were supposed to end up all along.

He drops you onto a mattress and undresses you, like a child. You surrender half-unconsciously to something you subsequently forget, subsequently uncertain as to whether it's what you actually came for, or if it was chance that drove you to seek refuge in the harbor of an old confidant. All you remember is that while you lay there clenching your teeth, it was like taking a shit, only the other way around. And with a lustful roar from your foulsmelling friend, it's as though all hope of happiness is sucked out of you, as though your insides are being drawn out through your rectum and that everything else is following after, all that is you, all that has been you these last few years, all you've enjoyed and looked forward to, all the things that have filled your days with light, and which are now being ripped out of you and discarded, like rubbish, like shit, like vile putrid pulp.

# A Mere Hint

SHE'S ASLEEP. You lie awake studying her face. Examining every last detail. For a little while you've nothing to be afraid of. So why aren't you happy? Now that nobody else can get to her? Now that it's just the two of you, alone together? Still, all you can feel is a crushing sensation, like the one you had on Sundays when you were a child, that feeling at night, when there was no way back, when a new week was to begin in a matter of hours, only back then there lay concealed in that bad feeling a notion of a time to come, innumerable years infinitely far away, but now there's no thought to the years ahead, now you can already make out the door to the end, and it's different from a future, it's the opposite of a future, it's a closed door that's going to open into the darkness. But as yet, she's just lying there, beside you, borne off by sleep, ignorant of the evil she has done and will do, so free beneath Oslo's rooftops, eaves and balconies, chimneys and spires, a young, tiny, and naked thing, she's a slender white speck, a touch, a mere hint, a glimpse of a possible person with an idolized, impossible dream within. And you feel loathing for sleep, which is allowed to possess her like this, to hold her so in thrall, so utterly abandoned, so unattainable for everything and everyone, if you could be that sleep . . . If you could be that, be something she completely lost herself in, is entirely absorbed with . . . And if that sleep you were could last forever . . . If you could be her sleep and she never woke again, then your happiness would last just as long . . . Through the layer of haze, the streetlights cast their reddish glow across her, making her once again radiant, solemn and mysterious. Her time has come. She lies there unaware that her big moment in life has now arrived. Everything is laid out. She can have anything she wants. Is there anything more evil than a woman who is worshipped? And tomorrow everything will continue as before, the humiliation and spite will begin anew, but in the meantime, for just a little while, she's above it all, above all of them, you included, she is the most beautiful and most important and most precious thing on earth, and deep down you know you're going to lose her.

*You had childhood in your hair blowing you clean*
*Winter clothed you in snow and human skin*
*You lay quietly awaiting living wind-up toys*
*If they came, you laughed*
*If not you could sleep*

*I said:*
*Just sleep,*
*Should they come, I will wake you*

Like a married couple you both arrive home each day, she from her studies, you from work, the two of you make dinner in the big kitchen on the first floor and eat at an old sideboard you bought at a flea market which is way too low to sit at, so you both hunch over as you eat. You think how love isn't supposed to be like this. But it's as though each of you is sitting inside a block of transparent jelly that words can't escape. In the evenings you go to the movies, or gigs, or both sit in the common room watching TV, unless you're invited to parties elsewhere in the dorm, usually in Kim's room, which he's decorated to look like a pub, or is it meant to look like a brothel, you're not sure.

He's doing you a favor letting you live there. And even though non-students aren't actually permitted and you constantly suffer looks from the students on your floor when you pass them in your Oslo Public Transport uniform, Kim holds his protective hand over both of you, as if it gives him particular satisfaction, having someone live there by his grace.

He and Amalie soon hit it off, the two of them often sit by themselves, something you're pleased about, to start with, because you like him and you're grateful for everything he's done for the two of you, and which only begins to bother you when it repeats itself for the fourth or fifth time, besides there's something more animated about them, when they sit together now, on several occasions you've heard Amalie burst out laughing.

All the same you exercise restraint. There's no way you're going to let him know what you think of it, you're not planning on giving the slightest hint of how it makes you feel when you see them with their heads close like that. You observe them surreptitiously. You pay attention to everything, every glance, every movement, every strained, innocent expression and every palpable no-it-was-nothing smile. Still you're friendliness personified toward the brute of a man who you know won't give up until he's slept with her, the woman who's going to be your wife, who is the love of your life, who is the Only One for you, something which the rest of the world doesn't seem to heed, on the contrary, it seems to make the rest of the world even more eager to conquer her, fuck her, sully her, drug her with charm so they can rape her. Still you don't express anything other than pure content over their growing friendship. Still you tell him straight out that Amalie is really glad she got to know him. Still you tell him, madness beyond all madness, THAT IT WOULD BE NICE IF HE DROPPED BY ONE EVENING FOR A CUP OF TEA!

Because he's not going to have any reason to think you're afraid of him. He's not going to get any impression at all that you're walking around in fear of what he and Amalie could conceivably get up to. He's not going to even consider the possibility that the thought could have crossed your mind that there could be anything between him and the love of your life.

One night you can't hold it back anymore, no matter how you persist in trying: As soon as you both come in the door and close it behind you, you let loose on her, take hold and shake her, roar at her, *if she was planning to try and make you believe that there was nothing between her and him . . . if she thinks you're so stupid that you don't realize that he's after her . . . if she thinks you don't see the looks they give one another . . . if she thinks you're blind to it . . . if she thinks it's credible, the fact that she hasn't cottoned on to the fact that he's aiming to score . . . what kind of idiot does she take you for to think they can carry on like that behind your back . . .* Amalie stands there in silence until you're finished. There's nothing visible in her countenance, nothing other than a sort of weary patience, as well as tristesse over having seen everything before, of not expecting any more from the world or from people, and their fumbling attempts to make it better. So, when she sees that you've calmed down, she gives your hair a gentle ruffle, as she would a child who has misbehaved, but who is already forgiven, and then she undresses and goes to bed.

She's so grown up, so like a woman all of a sudden. You see that rueful expression in her eyes: like a mother despairing of her son, who has disappointed her, but whom she knows she needs to stand by no matter what. That's how it is. She's grown bigger, you've grown smaller. She's matured and become a woman, you've shrunk and become a kid. She's at her most beautiful, you're at your most stupid. She's resolved, she stands in the light of her transfiguration and looks at you, as though from above.

The Seychelles, you think, sun, sea, warm beaches, no one the two of you know, no one to disturb you, no intrusions from any quarter, just you and Amalie, focusing on one another, on the only thing that matters, everything else miles and miles away, she just has to finish her education, and in the meantime you can wait, you can work and earn money, put by enough for the trip, which will be expensive, and then you can both go (never to return again). Turtles, coconuts, tea, and sweet potatoes, you've read, the rupee the only legal tender, maybe you could get married there, she has said yes after all, she said yes ages ago, all you need to do is remind her of it someday when you're standing in the coconut grove, and then go straight to the nearest priest. On a picture you've cut out and hung on the wall above the stereo, there's a native woman standing on a beach, right between two black boulders, they're smooth, polished, and strangely shaped, like two enormous curtains of stone: sometimes, when you look at it, you get the idea that it's you and Amalie standing there.

Beside the photo from the Seychelles hangs a poster, a reproduction of a painting by Salvador Dalí, where a fried egg hangs floating above a deserted landscape, tied up by a string. You were almost more taken aback by the title than you were by the picture the first time you saw it. And without being quite sure how it happened, it became a kind of refrain for you and her, a secret password you both had, which opened the door every time it locked. "Fried Egg on a Plate without the Plate," one of you would say each time either one of you wanted the conversation to take a different course, and then the other had to quickly change the subject (such was the law that must be obeyed). You found the picture in one of the books in Amalie's father's atelier, the cover was made from some strange, coarse material similar to burlap wallpaper, on the front was the name of the artist in big letters, and of all the pictures in it, this was the one which made the most impression on you. And you remember thinking of your father as you sat there for the first time studying it, how with a kind of ghastly delight you had attempted to imagine what he would have said if he had seen it.

You drop by a travel agency and when you get home, you draw up a budget, complete with traveling expenses, living expenses, detailed estimates of how much both of you would use on food and other necessities, with what you've saved up to now you're probably a third of the way there already. But when you show it to her in the evening (the lecture must have finished hours ago, where has she been?) she's not interested, gives the sheet a fleeting glance and hands it back, and when you ask what she thinks, she answers it will probably end up being a lot more expensive. "You always spend more money than you think you will," she says, and then goes into the bathroom. She's gone a long time. You're completely at a loss. It's like she's forgotten everything, doesn't remember all the things you talked about, even though the Seychelles was her idea, even though it was she who talked you into it and not the other way around. The brochure you brought home looks completely ridiculous lying there on the table, like a comic in a pile of newspapers. And when she finally appears in the doorway, you see it right away, the change that has occurred, her expression, her entire face, something has happened, as though many days, several weeks had passed from her having left the room to her coming back. She remains standing in the doorway.

"What is it?" you ask. "Has something happened?"

She takes a moment before closing the door, and you still can't figure out what you're supposed to be reading in her face, it could be fear just as much as unfettered joy. What kind of secret does she have that she can't manage to hide? What is it she's summoning up the courage to tell you? That she's seen Doberman again? That she's once again allowed herself to be led into temptation, has once again been unable to resist, has once again willingly allowed herself to be led, allowed herself to be fucked, sneered and grinned while she allowed herself to be defiled? Or is it something about her and Kim? Is she going to tell you that it's already happened? That they've already got around to it? That he's already been inside her? That she's already straddled him and taken pleasure in it?

"I haven't got it," she says. "I should've got it over a week ago, but I haven't."

In your trepidation over what she was going to say, you don't understand a word.

She looks at you and says: "I think I'm pregnant."

The words reach you but you still don't understand what she's saying, what's happened to her, why's she standing there like that . . . Is she happy? Or is she afraid? Worried? About what? About you? About what you'll say? Or is there something else, something much worse behind it? Is that why she's so scared? Is that why she's reluctant to say it? And from somewhere you hear yourself say: "By who?"

She stands there with the same expression. For a moment you're unsure if you actually said it or not. You move toward her, but then she raises her arm, her fingers splayed at you like a strange twisted star, like an instrument of torture: she doesn't lower it until you take a step back. She looks at you as though you were a stranger, someone who's entered the room illegally. Then she's released from her fear, as she recognizes the stranger standing there, as she realizes it's only you. She places the hand she lifted to halt you on her stomach, as though there were already a small bump there, as though she can already feel something moving.

And there's something in her eyes unlike anything you've ever seen there before, holding something more than she could relate to you, something big, overwhelming and paralyzing, more than she can manage to express. And when you see this look, when you see these eyes, the eyes of your sweetheart, whose gaze holds you tight, you feel a plunging sensation go through you. Your thoughts are brimming over, so many at once it's impossible to separate them from one another, you don't even know if they're all yours, it doesn't feel like it, it feels like every thought in existence, everything being thought at this moment in the world is flowing through you, a raging torrent forcing itself forward and washing away all that is you, all that is yours. It fills you up completely. Then it subsides. And then the tears come, even before Amalie has said a word. As though the final fierce pressure of the flood forces them out of you. And with the crying you return, sinking back into your own body, the tears streaming down, you're so weak anything could perforate you, a fly alighting on your arm would sink into your flesh. You're completely drained of energy, drained of intelligence. You sit on the floor weeping, in complete silence. Lips contorted, tears washing over your teeth, you're vaguely aware of Amalie approaching you, placing her arm around your neck. You try to say something to her, but are incapable of making yourself understood, not with the seething in your throat. Then, gradually, the room closes in around you. The white walls. The posters. The fried egg on a plate without the plate. The scent of Amalie's perfume. Amalie on her knees in front of you with her arms around you. You respond in an embrace. She pulls you back, up from the night and back into the day. The sobbing abates. What triggered it is gone. Something has raged through you and then moved on. You don't know what it was. You don't want to know what it was. Perhaps it was nothing. But for a moment you were one with the world. A world impossible to bear.

It looks like a duvet from a dollhouse where someone's been murdered in bed, the object she's waving in front of your face. At first you're as relieved as she is. But when the two of you have gone to bed and you hear her breathing fall further and further into a regular rhythm, it seems more and more obscene to you, the utter delight she displayed. Is she *so* overjoyed that she's not going to have a baby with you after all? Is it *so* intense, the relief in knowing there's no new life on its way, created from equal parts of you and her?

"Are you meeting Kim?" you ask, even though it's an entirely unreasonable thing to say, but it just slips out, like a strong, thin jet from a dam about to burst: she's taking such pains in deciding what to wear and she still hasn't said a word about where she's going, so you had to say something, you had to try and get it out of her somehow. And either she didn't hear what you said, or she's pretending she didn't hear, because when she's finally finished in front of the mirror, she just walks over, gives you a peck on the cheek and says she might be late so you needn't wait up. The two of you had been at a party in Kim's room the night before, a lot of people had been there, a lot of drink had been taken, everything was swimming in front of your eyes, but there was one clear spot in all that was turbid, a clear spot that was Amalie, you constantly caught a glimpse of her and lost sight of her again, and every time you saw her, the person sitting beside her became more discernable, and eventually he grew so clear that you could see who it was, and you finally realized it was Kim sitting there, that it was him sitting there feeding off her every single time you caught sight of her, he'd been sitting there with her all night, the last thing you'd seen was the two of them together, and the way you remember it, it was as though Kim had been much bigger than her, that he'd grown larger each time you looked at them, that he had steadily grown during the evening until eventually he'd become over twice her size, which was perhaps not so strange, with the size of the bites he was taking out of her, just like she was on her way to disappearing inside of him, becoming part of his body, something indistinguishable from the rest of him when he finally got up and left and began to wander the streets of Oslo at daybreak, ten stories high, with what he still hadn't devoured of Amalie hanging from his jaws, an arm here and a foot there, dangling out of time with the monster's heavy steps, which made the whole city shake and left a trail of black zigzags in the crushed asphalt.

Amalie strikes up new acquaintances in her course, is a part of something bigger right away, something new and lively, something tempting and enticing. And you notice how it's becoming easier for her every time, to say that she's going out, how her explanations are growing vaguer and vaguer. "Just heading out with a few people." She begins to do whatever she likes, as if she had a moral right, after having put up with you for so long. All that's new ignites ardor in her. The World is calling her. There are more appealing things than an evening in the common room in front of the TV, or a two-man backgammon tournament, or yet another night by the stereo, together with you, happy and carefree in the paradise of endlessly repeated favorite records._

You hear the name Marianne. At first you don't take much notice of it. One of many. One of countless others in the new daily life of Amalie that doesn't include you. Not before you hear it for the tenth or twentieth time and you suddenly become aware of its piercing ring, like a wholly new word from that voice you know so well, or thought you knew, a word her lips had never formed to pronounce before, but which now plops out of her mouth all the time. It sounds utterly grotesque. It's like a dissonance in the wonderful music you've been living with. And too late you realize you've already heard it a hundred times, a thousand times, Marianne, Marianne, Marianne, Marianne, Marianne, Marianne, Marianne, Marianne, Marianne, Marianne, Marianne, Marianne, Marianne, Marianne, Marianne, Marianne, Marianne, Marianne, Marianne, Marianne, Marianne, Marianne, Marianne, Marianne, Marianne, Marianne, Marianne, Marianne, Marianne, Marianne, like some vulgar word in a foreign language she, your sweetheart, has begun taking lessons in, without you knowing about it: all of a sudden she's sitting there in front of you, without you having paid attention to what's been going on, speaking *Mariannish*!

Marianne. Marianne. Marianne. Marianne. Marianne. Marianne. Marianne. Marianne. Marianne. Marianne. Marianne. Marianne. Marianne. Marianne. Marianne. Marianne. Marianne. Marianne. Marianne. Marianne. Marianne. Marianne. Marianne. Marianne. Marianne. As though she's taken possession of Amalie, as though she were on the way to filling her up completely. They form a new unit, inseparable, as if she (Amalie) now solely speaks to you by quoting her (Marianne), that no statement leaves her without support in some opinion Marianne holds or has expressed.

There's a debate night at the Student Union that some friends of hers have helped to organize, and there's an unpleasant maternal ring to her voice when she suggests that you could come along, the way she puts it, *that it would do you good to get a bit more involved*, as though it were a matter of making up for some omission on your part, that she thinks you've pottered around long enough in your own world, that you need to open your eyes to "the real world out there." What the hell is out there in the world to interest you, when there's more than enough to worry about in the world the two of you share in here? You sit looking at the others around the table while a discussion takes place on the stage: Amalie's new friends, her new clique, they look so ridiculous, so self-important, all sitting there trying to look serious. And you look at Amalie and try to work out where she fits in. And you're baffled, you can't understand what she's doing here, can't comprehend what she's got to gain from this, you can't manage to see it as anything other than a step backwards, for her, this gem, to sit among these cheap imitations, for her to assume this pseudo-serious mask, for her to join this loathsome crowd who are so utterly *banal*.

Just then she looks in your direction, the panel have opened up for questions from the audience, and it's almost as if there's an element of reproach in the look she's sending you. Is it because you won't take the floor? Is it because you aren't showing enough interest? Is it because you're just sitting there, like a halfwit, instead of launching yourself into the debate, putting forward a few points, getting torn into what's been said from the stage? Then she turns to the one sitting beside her, who you've yet to be introduced to, but who you realize is Marianne, and they exchange fleeting eye contact, a knowing look, as between two people who share a secret. And a terrible thought takes hold of you, that *that's what couples do*, it's the kind of look lovers send one another. And that it's you who ought to have received it, you she ought to have looked at in that way, the two of you who ought to be sitting there exchanging furtive glances and knowing expressions to each other about how insufferable it is sitting there, the two of you who ought to be looking forward to being alone together again and being able to speak your minds.

But that look, it's just been given to someone else. She's shared what she's really thinking with another. She's rolled her eyes to someone who is not you.

Your head feels roasting hot and you start to sweat. The walls move toward one another. The large room begins to contract, becoming unbearably cramped, as though you're all sitting inside a little cube. You gasp for air. Anyone looks your way now and you'll break down. Anyone asks you a question now and you'll burst apart from the inside, explode right before their eyes.

Fried egg on a plate without the plate! you think. FRIED EGG ON A PLATE WITHOUT THE PLATE!

Afterwards, in the cool freedom of the autumn evening, you stand talking, Amalie and Marianne and you. They want to go to the concert that's on at the same place later on, you come up with an excuse not to stay. And you're not sure, but you thought you saw visible relief pass across Amalie's face when you said it. You talk about this and that, then you leave. Marianne gives you a funny look when you say good-bye, you think about it the whole way home, but can't manage to work it out.

Only later does it come to you: *It was the look of one who knows.* Of one who's been told. You didn't perceive it then, but you grasped it later. Amalie has told Marianne everything. She, Amalie, has violated the confidence you share. She's initiated another. She no longer feels tied. She's broken away. She's already begun to withdraw. She's asked another person to help her get away.

You try to think good thoughts. You seize upon every sign of concrete evidence. But it makes no difference what she says or does. The images from within subdue the images from without. She can be standing naked in front of you, her arms outstretched, and all you see is betrayal, deceit and flirtation. She smiles to you, that wonderful smile which once awoke the person within in you, and you feel nauseous at the thought of who else this smile will be directed at, that day you can't manage to hold onto it any longer. That wonderful, irresistible smile which is yours, yours, yours . . . right up until it's somebody else's. She caresses your neck and you think: What others will you stroke this way, with such tenderness, with such pleasure and delight? In the darkness of the movie theatre, her hand groping its way down along to your crotch and squeezing it, and you think: if someone else had been sitting here, you'd be doing the same thing, wouldn't you? You celebrate your birthday, when you wake up in the morning there's twenty red roses lying spread across the duvet, and you think: you'd probably like there to be thirty or forty roses lying there, and that the guy you were together with was twice as old, that he was a mature man, one with no insecurities, one who was assured in every respect, one who displayed calm in any given situation, one who could show you the world, who could introduce you to everything unfamiliar, who could tell you, with a worldly air, all you needed to know.

In the evening, she treats you to marzipan cake at one of the nicest cafés in town, and while you sit there holding one another's hands, you think: you'd so much rather have arrived arm in arm with a real man, a mannered man with expensive habits, one you never needed to pick up the check for, one who ordered for both of you, no matter where you were, one who treated the waiter in a condescending fashion, one who didn't put up with anything, one who didn't hesitate in sending the food back if there was something wrong with it, if there was so much as a tiny speck on the edge of the plate, or if the vegetables were undercooked, or if the wine didn't taste as it should.

And you think about Doberman, who took her so hard and with such brutality (like nobody has done since), and who no doubt still lives in the city, and whom there's a reasonable chance of her bumping into one day, what kinds of feelings this meeting will give rise to, what kind of wonderful forbidden feelings, and how tempted she will be to relive it, to get carried away once more, let him take control, like she did that time, come what may, take his huge cock inside her one more time, like a sorely missed scepter, like a holy relic. And you picture it, how they set off, horny and in a hurry, to his flat, how he takes her by the hand and leads her up the stairs, how he sticks his tongue in her mouth as soon as he's closed the door behind them, how he tears off her clothes, how he shoves her down on the sofa, how he fucks her hard and furiously, without saying a word, how he comes at the same time as her, how he lies on top of her for a few moments, in her embrace, until she pushes him off and gets up from the couch, dresses quickly and leaves him, sated, liberated, happy, as she skips lightly down the stairs and through the gloomy yard, out into the open. Out in the open and home to you, flushed, while behaving as though nothing had happened. And if they didn't do it, it still wouldn't make any difference, because the dream of doing it, the thought of how it would be if they did, that would still have been stirred within her, that would still pursue her, that would never quite leave her, never quite let go, the thought of the most sumptuous of them all, the hardest and most brutal of them all, that would always be lying there dormant.

You hear her voice coming from the kitchen on the first floor. She's laughing. What's she doing here? From what you gathered she had lectures all day? You begin climbing the stairs while listening carefully. Then you halt, standing tensed with your hand on the bannisters. You go back down, treading gingerly, one step at a time, the way one tests bathwater with one's toes.

You hear a deep mutter, then her laughter again, bubbly and carefree. You begin walking toward the kitchen, but stop up every time the voices reach you, whether his or hers. Doberman! you think. He's finally found her! You pause by the door for a while, your back against the door frame, hear Amalie laugh, a man's voice beneath hers, hardly getting a word in she's so eager to speak.

Then her voice suddenly becomes clear, like a successful restoration of an old tape recording, and you hear her say something which should only be said between the two of you, words she shouldn't utter to anyone other than you.

You lean forward cautiously and peek in. Amalie is standing with her back to you. Who is it sitting on the kitchen counter in front of her? And what are they up to? Are they kissing? No, they still seem to be talking. He's trying to impress her, doing some kind of impersonation while swaying from side to side. Now he's saying something. You strain to hear. But it doesn't matter: you can see the understanding between them, how easily they relate to one another, how naturally they behave together. And then Amalie turns around. You jerk back from the gap in the doorway. The last thing you saw, although you're not sure, was Kim's hand on Amalie's shoulder, as though he wanted to hold her back, prevent her from going, twist her close, lock her in his grip, press his mouth to hers, open her lips with his tongue and force his way inside her.

If it had turned out that she had been pregnant, you think, how would things be then, what would her attitude have been, to Kim, to Marianne and to all the others on her course? If she had been walking around carrying what was to be your baby and hers, would there be unpleasant surprises awaiting you when you returned home a little earlier than usual? Would she have had any interest at all in the others? Would there be the slightest iota left of the dream about Doberman? Would there then be anything else that counted, that was of worth, that was of concern to her, other than the both of you, the two of you together, and the little one on the way? If it had turned out to be growing inside her all the same, would there be anything left in this world to fret about?

Amalie is out with some friends, you don't know which. You're sitting alone in the common room watching a movie that makes you completely forget both time and place. Only a long time after it's finished do you realize you've been sitting in the dark, that no lights are on, and your hands on the armrests are blue in the glow of the screen, just like a zombie's sitting there. You remain motionless for a long time, you watch a news broadcast where the newsreader's mouth moves out of synch with what he's saying, after the main stories there's a piece about a school band traveling by bus to a city in Germany. But eventually you get up from the chair, turn off the TV and go up to the room, drag a chair over to the window, sit down with your elbows on the windowsill and start keeping an eye out for her. The intersection below, with the white pedestrian crossing and the strict system of traffic lights continuously changing from green to red and from red to green, seems utterly meaningless now nobody's there to conform to it.

The yellow facades are already becoming brighter when she suddenly appears out of nowhere, and hurries from the pavement across the street and into the building. She gives a start and lets out a little cry when she lets herself in and discovers you sitting there. After you're both in bed, she asks what you've been doing while she was out. You tell her you watched a movie, and that it made a real impression on you, you say it was about true love, and that it was the first time you've seen true love depicted with such authenticity and to such effect on film. And then you relate the plot to her, describing the protagonist in detail, how he slowly but surely goes mad because he gets it into his head that his wife is unfaithful, although it's never made clear if she really is or if the whole thing is all just a product of the man's imagination coupled with a series of unfortunate coincidences, all the same he just can't stop thinking about it and in a brutal final act he first kills the man he believes to be his wife's lover, then his wife, before finally putting the gun in his mouth and shooting himself.

The hand that had been resting on your chest slips away. And you can hear by her voice that she's scared when she asks:

"And you thought that was good?" You're not sure what she's referring to, if it's the film or the actions of the husband, you can just hear by her voice that she's afraid and you understand that it's what you've said that's scared her. The two of you lie there in silence for a while, as daybreak spreads through the room and birdsong begins, like a tribute to something that no longer exists.

"I've been thinking about something," she says, eventually. "About some changes."

And it's as though her voice still holds some of the fear from before, fear and something else besides, the opposite, something bold, something audacious, something brazen. And when she continues it's like you recognize Marianne's voice. You hear that they are her words, her formulations, hear that she's the one lying there talking, she's the one speaking on behalf of Amalie.

"I'd like if we tried out a slightly different arrangement," says Marianne. "Where we have a little more freedom than we have now. Where it doesn't have to be just us, necessarily, the whole time. That if something happens, or we meet somebody, then we can go with it. Without it having to ruin anything. If you know what I mean? That we don't need to feel so tied down. That we don't always need to take things into consideration and never get to do anything at all."

A brief silence.

And then: "What do you think?"

And still you lie there, alongside her, the hideous friend of your sweetheart, in the harsh light, unable to say a word, unable to lift a finger, almost unable to draw breath.

You walk together to the train station, you've been to the cinema, Amalie and Marianne and you, the two of them are going on into town, you're going down to the subway to do a nightshift, and the entire time prior to you taking leave of one another you're thinking: *I'm not going to say anything! I'm not going to say anything! I'm not going to say anything! I'm not going to say anything!* But you saw how she did herself up, how she dressed up before you left, you see how attractive and sexy she is as she walks along beside you, you get the scent of her perfume and think that perhaps she's seen Doberman, that he's the one who put the idea in her head, that he's the reason she wants free rein, in case a chance with him should arise, all the same you exhort yourself: *you're not going to say anything! you're not going to say anything! you're not going to say anything!* There's a raw smell of sea in the city air, mingling with the scent of Amalie's perfume, and the sky is luminous and swollen, saturated with green and blue, like the belly of a fly about to lay its eggs. And just as you've given each other a hug and said your good-byes and they're turning to go, you shout, with as much scorn in your voice as you can muster: "Good luck with the new arrangement then!"

You watch Amalie stop, see the disbelief in her eyes. Marianne, standing beside her, stares in surprise, first at Amalie, then at you. And for a moment you stand there meeting Amalie's gaze, without knowing what it is you want to express, whether it's anger or despair, menace, caution, or just downright fear. But it's as though it's not you standing there, it's as though that ridiculous uniform doesn't belong to you, that it's another person standing there, someone you are inside of, someone you're looking through the eyes of, some poor wretch who's standing there with an expression of complete dejection, gaping after the two girls walking along the pavement, hand in hand.

She begins to dress more provocatively. She stands humming while she fixes herself up to go out. She's hung up a yellow sheet of paper with the lyrics of "Don't Fence Me In" by Cole Porter beside the mirror. Every line in it is an insult, as though Marianne had leaned in and whispered what to write into Porter's ear. You try not to look at it, attempt to avert your gaze, but when you wake up at night, you know it by heart. She's friendly, forthcoming, always cheerful, in good form and full of energy. She's beautiful, more beautiful than you've ever seen her, you feel something loosen within you every time you see her. When you reach out for her, she doesn't reject you. No, she takes your hand, kisses it, or strokes her cheek with it, or squeezes it affectionately, but swiftly. When you try to kiss her, she lets you, doesn't push you away, but doesn't reciprocate either, merely responds with a friendly peck, a smack on the lips and a pat on the cheek. You hug her, you hold her tight against you, and she stands patiently waiting for you to relax your grip. You touch her up, feel her breasts, hold them gently in your hands, and she allows them to rest there as long as you want, rest in your trembling grasp, before twisting herself free with a friendly smile. Being cheerful, carefree and easy are the hallmarks of Amalie's new world, her "new arrangement." She flirts with you, sends you furtive glances and makes sly innuendos. *She preens herself for you, without it meaning a thing.* She preens herself for you, the same as she does for all the others. She flirts with all of them, you *included.* You've become one of them, one of the others, one of all those she knows and whom she makes eyes at. She's just as cheeky, unabashed and flirtatious with you as she is with them. From now on, you're one of many who admire her, one in a long line of men, gilding her with their hungry looks.

You're at a birthday party one of the girls in the building is having, when you catch a glimpse of Marianne, surreally present
among all the people, you need to look a couple of times, before
you're sure it's her. It galls you to see her there, your annoyance
doubled by the thought of the special treatment (on Amalie's
part) that has gained her entry. Much later in the night she comes
over and immediately starts interrogating you, asking why you're
with Amalie, asking if you love her, in which case if you do, are
you sure that's what you're actually doing, what love means to
you, what your understanding of a relationship is, questions you
have no clue about, nor why she, of all people, should be asking
you, and when you finally get a chance to begin to respond, her
eyes narrow, clearly preparing for the worst, the most deranged
guff from a sick mind, her gaze like a chink under a closed door.
She continues grilling you until Amalie comes over, she's been to
get another bottle of wine, and she pours it, first for Marianne,
then for you, and then she puts her arm around Marianne, raises
her glass and says: "To the future!"

*To the future* . . . What the fuck has she got in mind? What kind
of plans are they busy hatching behind your back? How long
has it been going on? What is it they have their eyes on? Are
they planning to run away? Escape from it all, crisscross the
continent, live as lesbians on the run, live life with complete
abandon? And you recall Amalie's mother and the woman she'd
been sitting draped around an entire evening, like a horny snake,
and whom she'd French kissed in full view of everyone, and you
think: she's probably inherited it, it's probably in her blood, she
can't stop herself, even if she really wanted to, she still wouldn't
be able to stop.

Still you lie beside one another in bed at night, still naked, she's peaceful, her breathing regular, you with your heart close to beating all the breath out of you, your chest close to tearing, your genitals ready to burst, your muddled brain under attack from an angry swarm of arguments for and against whether you should lift your hand and dare touch her. The times you do venture, you almost pass out when you feel her skin: it's as though everything that's been lost is restored by the slightest, most fleeting touch.

One night you can't stand it any longer and you roll on top of her, force her legs apart and enter her, clutch her tightly, fill your mouth with her breasts, your fingers frantically exploring all that's familiar: buttocks, thighs, belly, shoulders, throat, feeling an irresistible urge to sink your teeth into her tits, scratch away, tear out hair and maul her. And then you come, and she still hasn't moved a muscle, she's just lain there, limp, like a blow-up doll and let you carry on until you were spent. Silently, with gritted teeth, you empty a huge wad of sperm into the dead body beneath you. And in an undertow of despair you collapse on top of her and lie there like a manhole cover, for a few seconds you have no idea where you are. Then you feel her arm move. A hand strokes you across the hair. A warm surge of hope flows through you. But then another hand comes into play, and together the two hands push you gently off, over to your side of the bed, where you lie on your back detached from the woman you've assaulted. And still not a sound escapes her lips, still she lies quite motionless beside you, as though asleep. And perhaps she is asleep? Perhaps she's been asleep the whole time. Been vaguely aware of someone having struggled his way inside her while she slept. Been vaguely cognizant of the semen being shot into her in her sleep. Been half-conscious as she eased the sweaty weight off her and slept on peacefully. Ashamed, you lift your hand to your nose and sniff her scent. And you think about what's now been deposited inside her, how it's probably running out in a thin streak from between her indifferent pudenda, and you think about the smell of her room, that night you made love for the first time, the cool sweat on the bedclothes, the chill in the night air from the open window, crisp clear autumn, the piercing sound from the venetian blinds, the wonderful weight of the body lying half on top of you, the warmth and sweat uniting you both, the happiness too great for the soul of one single boy to bear.

The two of you stand outside on the little balcony smoking. It hasn't been long since she took it up, her motions still not quite practiced, like those of a little girl playing grown-up. She seems nervous: because she's afraid I'm going to start asking her questions? Or restless: because she can't wait to be on her way again, out to all that awaits her? She takes short drags of the cigarette, blowing the smoke out right away, as if her mouth can't stand being filled with it. Her eyes rove, never settling on one spot, as though she were following an insect with them, and she doesn't say anything, even though you've both been standing there a while, and to think how she used to babble away. She puts out the cigarette, long before it's finished, it looks like a deformed finger in the ashtray. She flashes you a smile that's impossible to read, opens the balcony door and goes inside.

And you can picture her, how she begins to run as soon as she's out of sight, how she snatches the yellow coat off the peg, hurries down the stairs, out onto the pavement, rushes through the streets with heart pounding and cheeks flushed, like a spring wind through the city, beautiful and unabashed, elated and glowing, borne along by a tingling, aching feeling of happiness in her arms and legs which tense all the muscles in her body and loose her like an arrow.

That's how she is: horny, happy and game for anything. That's how she is out there. That was the way she was when you met. That was how she won your heart. Now it's the domain of others. You don't even need to bother trying! Everything is hostile and glowering. The circle is drawing in. Her circle. The society of the living. The ones who'll enter into anything. With anybody. The ones who'll take what life has to offer. It's not *you* she needs any longer, it's *that*. And you realize that what you know about her is a just a thin, thin costume, pulled over a gorgeous voluptuous body which is under wraps and in reality has never belonged to you, never will belong to you, and will forever be reserved for anybody else who may come her way. You wish the real world didn't exist.

# Doberman

You've just made love. Amalie is lying with her head on your shoulder dozing, you're lying looking up at the white ceiling which is like the sky above, difficult to say how close or how far it is, and you think: *This is me! I'm the one lying here! I'm the one lying here together with her! That's mine, that arm she's resting on! The most beautiful girl in the world is lying here with half her body on top of mine!*

You're startled as her hand, monstrously large, sweeps across your vision. She rolls off you, lies on her back beside you for a while, then raises herself up onto her elbows and looks at you with a peculiar expression. And then she suggests that you tell each other about all the people you've been with before the two of you got together. You agree to it, feeling a tingling in your stomach as soon as the decision is made, and together you resolve to tell each other everything, everything you've done with other people, from the least significant to the most important, neither of you are to hold back at all, not one single secret is to remain.

But it's her who has most to disclose, you only have a few fairly innocuous incidents to contribute, some covert necking, brief groping and fumbling, the girlfriend you had last summer, some instances of arousal which never reached their natural outcome. While she, the lovely Amalie . . . *and for a moment you're terrified by the thought of what you might hear.*

First, to your relief, she tells you she never slept with that big, burly guy, whose name was Dag, and even though they did do pretty much everything you can otherwise, it doesn't affect you in the slightest as she lists it off, all of it, anaesthetized as you are in the happy knowledge of the last bastion remaining intact.

You sit at each end of the mattress until you're both done. But afterwards, you can see it in her face, you know she hasn't told you everything, that she's holding something back, something she's reluctant to tell you. It takes a long time for her to get it out. You have to coax and cajole. But then it comes. You sit there in silence and listen to her story from start to finish.

It was last summer, right after the breakup with Dag the bear. Amalie and a friend had traveled into Oslo to visit her friend's brother. And one night they'd gone to a concert. They only got past the bouncers by the skin of their teeth, but once inside they soon found themselves being taken care of by an older guy decked out in leather and wearing makeup, who, it turned out, was the vocalist in the band that was going to play. Excited and in high spirits, they had allowed themselves to be bought one drink after another. Amalie's friend had got drunk and had to go home, but Amalie stayed on, up until the concert finished, and afterwards the members of the band took her along to a party back at the leather-clad guy's place. And then she didn't remember much more until the apartment was empty of people, and she was lying naked on a sofa with the vocalist standing over her stripping off. They had had sex several times during the night. At one point she had to get onto her knees on the floor while she took him in her mouth. This was at daybreak, and suddenly she'd grown afraid, and when he went to the bathroom a little while later to shower, she had got dressed in a hurry and gone out the door, run down the stairs and through the streets, rushing home to her friend and her brother, who fortunately left her in peace and didn't demand any explanation for her disappearance.

A look of anxious relief spreads across her features when she's finished. She looks at you, imploringly. It's as though she's waiting for you to deliver a verdict. But you don't know what to say, the only thing you feel is nausea, a stinging dread in your heart, a feeling of disgust that you know you'd be wise to conceal from her. If you're able. If you manage to resist. If your chest doesn't explode and everything come spilling out someday.

You ask her some questions, where the concert was held, what the name of the band was, what his name was, this lead singer in leather, you feel an overwhelming urge to find out all the details. At the same time you're terrified of what these details will allow you to visualize. It becomes more and more vivid, clearer and clearer with every new piece of information you drag out of her. And you hate what you see. The vision of her on the sofa. Horny. Drunk. Naked. Vulgar. Giggling. With that dirty old man on top of her. He was twice her age and called himself Doberman, that was his stage name, and the walls of his apartment, they were green, they'd been decorated with hundreds of pornographic pictures. He had asked to take her up the ass too, but she hadn't wanted to. "But doing it the usual way, you liked that?" you ask, and it smarts in your throat as you say it, it feels like you're going to choke every time a new question works its way up your gullet and out of your mouth. You ask and ask and ask. And are disgusted by the wavering, slightly stammering answers she gives, the way she replies, shamefaced and risible at the same time. And you think: *I'm the only reason she's ashamed, if I hadn't been here she'd have delighted in these memories.*

You can picture it. His sofa, where it was in the room, what kind of color it was, the shape of it, what position Amalie was lying in when he entered her the first time and how they dozed off, entwined in one another between each fuck. Where on the floor she found her clothes again. The entire apartment, you reconstruct it like a crime scene. And you continue the cross-examination. What they had been talking about earlier that evening. What the concert had been like. If she'd liked the music. If he was a good singer. What she had told her friend and her friend's brother when she got back the next morning. How she had felt. How had it felt thinking about it afterwards. If it was true that she had been afraid. In what way had she been afraid? Afraid he was going to rape her? But wasn't there maybe a bit of a thrill in that too? Was she positive that deep down she didn't want that? If she has seen him since? If she's thought about getting in touch? If she's ever found herself wanting to relive the experience, look him up and let him know she was game? If she thought of it as something bad, what had happened, or as something good? If she regretted it or was happy about it? If she? If she? If she?

Then the two of you make love, with more ferocity than usual, both randy and unrestrained, as though it were important to get it done. You receive a scratch mark across your chest, a red, jagged streak beside one nipple. Afterwards you sit naked and hold one another, like you did on the veranda at Gunnar's party that night. You stay like that for a long time, without saying anything, faces buried in the hollow of each other's necks, arms and legs tightly intertwined. But all you can think about is the guy in leather. The image of him and Amalie, bodies twisted into all kinds of strange positions. Amalie on her knees on the floor, like a dog. The words he whispers in her ear as he takes her. And when you take a look around, you're back in the scumbag's apartment: the filthy sofa standing over in the corner, and in front of you, on the carpet, their clothes are lying together in an abhorrent bundle.

When you awake at dawn you're all woozy, and you sit up in bed staring for a long time before the room falls into place around you. But a creeping unease in your body tells you something's not right. You glance around. In the pale light everything has changed, somebody must have moved the two of you while you both slept. You turn to look at her. She's lying on her back with her mouth open and one arm outstretched, prized away from this world, a faint whistling coming from her nose. You look at her and know that the world has changed. That what was present only a few hours ago will never return, that something's been taken away, been removed, and that something new, something you didn't know existed, has come to take its place.

You've browsed through her LP collection countless times, without taking any particular notice of this one, but now the letters on its spine beat upon your pupils like tiny hammers: BAR MALDOROR, you read, and you know you've seen it before, you recognize the cover. And sure enough, there he stands, Doberman, just as you feared, on the back, dressed in black leather, his arms outstretched in a priest-like pose, as if he were blessing the other members of the band. A diabolic priest. A black-clad devil. A lecherous fiend. By blessing them and everything they stand for he's mocking you. He's standing there with an ironic sneer staring right at you, you fool, you little shit, you fucking would-be civil servant in your newly ironed shirt.

That was probably how he looked, you think, no doubt with that selfsame expression, as Amalie stood there undressing for him. He has an upside down cross hanging over his bulging crotch. And you're aware of having looked at it before, of having stood with the album in your hands several times, yes, you've stood there studying the cover while she's been looking at you, you've held it in your hands, right next to her, and admired it, *you've stood there thinking that it was cool!*

There's something almost illegible written in the bottom corner, which at first you take for graffiti on the wall behind them, but which you now see is written in felt pen. You hold it up to the light, and from the glimmer of the remains of what's written in marker, you make out: TO AMALIE. SMILE!

You're standing with the album in your hands when Amalie comes in. She doesn't notice it at first, or pretends not to notice. But when you hold it up to show her, without saying anything, she laughs and looks away. "Have you been listening to it?" she asks, trying to smooth over her nervousness with a light, casual tone. You don't reply. She avoids eye contact. Her uncertainty satisfies you and it scares the hell out of you.

"Are you going to put it on or what?" she says, finally. What's she up to? Is she trying to pretend she doesn't know who it is? Pretend she doesn't know why you've taken it out, why you're standing there with it in your hands showing it to her like that? She begins to orbit you, doing this and that, still not showing any of the emotions that the sight of the record must have brought about in her. But perhaps it's joy rather than sorrow? You follow her with your eyes for a while. And then disgorge your fresh questions: How was it he'd given her a signed copy of the record, if, as she said, she'd never seen him since? *Her: He gave it to me at the gig!* You: How did you manage to bring the record with you if you got dressed in such a hurry and ran off? *Her: It was just lying there, together with my clothes!* You: Why did you take it with you, after all, you said you were scared? *Her: I guess I didn't really think it over!* You: Why haven't you got rid of it? Why did you hang onto it, if you were so frightened? *Her: I like their songs! I think they're good!* You: How could you listen to it, after what happened? *Her: I don't think about it! I listen to the music!* You: Why don't you throw it away, now that you know that I know about it? *Her: Throw away a record? Are you mad?*

You tell yourself they don't matter, the things she did before you met, who she was with, who she did one thing or the other with, as long as you're the one she's together with now, as long as it's you she's doing it with now. You tell yourself: Let the past be the past! What does it matter if she's been horny and happy together with other men, when it's just you she's horny and happy with now? What do you care what feelings she *has had*, when you know what feelings she *has*? Are you not the luckiest eighteen-year-old on earth? Are the two of you not the happiest couple on earth? Don't the two of you form the unbreakable core of true love?

You see him in your dreams. You see him when you're awake. You see him everywhere. Standing tall, feet apart, a broad grin on his face, his hands at his sides and his dick raised like a spear in front of him, Amalie on her knees, like a dutiful servant, a worshipper of the divine, naked and in a drunken stupor, game for everything, up for anything, randy Amalie and leering Doberman, thrusting, grinding Doberman, the one who lured your girl, *although there didn't seem to be much luring necessary* . . . the one who lured and assaulted her, *although she obviously didn't regard it as such* . . . the one who assaulted and destroyed her, *even though she didn't realize it herself, but perhaps that was part of the destruction* . . . ?

You try to look away, but the images keep coming, spewed up from the underworld. Every joy you experience with your sweetheart up here is poisoned by a pang from down there. You both sit in a café drinking tea, *and you insist on finding out how many rounds Doberman bought her friend and her* . . . You lie entwined around one another in bed, *and you ask if they also held one another after they'd fucked for the first time* . . . She puts your thumb in her mouth and sucks on it, *and you want to know if she has done the same with his* . . .

It's like having a job, in addition to school and life with Amalie, a covert occupation. It's as though you're living two lives, one in daylight, together with Amalie, the other down in the depths, in the underworld, together with Doberman. There's an enormous amount of archival work involved: for every fresh piece of information you find, there's something new you need to know, which won't leave you in peace until you've managed to unearth it, and when Amalie isn't able to tell you, you need to find the answer out yourself on the basis of what you know, so you imagine what you don't know, all the things she won't come out and say, because she knows that they'd hurt you if she told you, that you wouldn't be able to take it, that you'd be utterly devastated when you realized how much she still relishes thinking about it even today, to what extent she simply couldn't be without it. And every time a smile plays on her lips, every time a small sigh of pleasure distorts those fantastic features, you visualize the terrible congress that has taken place. Every time she's lost in thought, every time you catch her with a faraway look, you take it for granted that it's memories from the green apartment of death she's deriving pleasure from.

The two of you take the train to Oslo, leaving home at dawn, and later in the day first catch sight of the boat, which resembles an apartment block, looming up high behind the ferry terminal and walkways. "There's Copenhagen," says Amalie. You buy tickets and go aboard, standing on the top deck as the boat leaves the quay, without having let anyone know where you're going, not the school, not your parents, and it's going to be at least another two days before you're home again. "Puh, they don't care," says Amalie when you ask her what she thinks they're going to say. No, you think, your parents probably don't. But mine. They're sitting at home waiting for me. They've already left no stone unturned.

The water in the fjord glitters, smaller craft appear and disappear according to where the light hits. The two of you stand at the furthest end of the deck, leaning against the railing, entrusting your faces to the wind and whatever grimaces result. Faster and faster it goes, the boat is a machine, you're the people commanding it, the sun is warm and on the lower deck people are gathered closely along the side in a grateful, colorful row.

"Amalie," you say. She's standing with her feet on the railings, leaned forward with her eyes closed and arms outstretched.

You stand looking at her.

"What is it?"

She lowers her arms, turns slowly and opens her eyes.

"Will you marry me?"

At first she doesn't react. Her hair is completely over to one side, she takes it in her hand, gathers it into a bun and places it behind the collar of her coat.

Then she smiles: "Of course I will!"

She puts her arms around you, you kiss, standing fused in the wind at the very end of the top deck, the sun shining, you form a Siamese figurehead traveling south, away from everything. Fried egg on a plate without the plate. The huge machine is working for you both, taking you where you want to go, the two of you deciding where the trip will lead. But the pause she took, before answering, the time she obviously needed to think it over before saying yes, you can already feel taking root, like yet another wicked tree in the pit of your stomach.

She doesn't want you. You want her but she doesn't want you. It's the first time it's happened. You stroke her across the shoulder and she recoils, wants to be left alone, looks the other way, over at something she doesn't want you to see. The zebra-striped panties are all she's wearing, she's so gorgeous that it's painful being so close to her. The bed rocks, the cabin is tiny, there's a curtain on the wall that makes it look as though there's a window there, you've been fooled several times and have drawn it, expecting to see the ocean.

"Who are you thinking about?" you ask, realizing immediately that you should have said "what" instead of "who," but now it's too late, and what does it matter: it was what you were thinking, so why wouldn't you say it?

She doesn't reply, just twists away from a new caress, even before your hand has touched her.

"Who are you thinking about?" you repeat.

A deep moan, in a tone that doesn't sound like her, comes from the other side of her back.

"Is it him?"

You're not sure but it sounds like she's crying.

"Is that why you don't want to?"

"Give it a break!" she sobs.

But you can't stop: "Are you thinking about Doberman?" Suddenly she turns, a wild expression on her face, eyes blood-shot, her features hardly recognizable and before you're able to react she's hit you in the face with her fist. The blows rain down, a cracking sound from your nose, something breaking and beginning to flow, and she doesn't let up until you start hitting back, she tumbles backward on the bed and before she's able to gather herself you're on top of her, she waves her arms like crazy, until eventually you get hold of both her wrists and force her onto her back. Even when you're tugging and yanking her panties off she resists, twisting and writhing in order to stop you. But finally she's naked and in the next moment you're inside her, blood spattering her stomach and tits, the whole of her being smeared, and for a second you think of something quite terrible. But then she settles down, she looks at you, she's glowing and then her calm passes over to you, becomes part of you. Your nose feels like it's twice as big, it's still dripping, dark red stars appearing everywhere on her body, making it look like her skin's about to tear. You both lie like that for a long time, in complete silence, and let the listing of the boat do the job for you.

When the boat docks in the morning you really just want to stay in the cabin, but the regulations, as you're informed over the PA system, require everyone to go on land. You both dress quickly, outside it's raining, a red tanker blocks the view as you exit the arrivals hall. You traipse up and down the streets, eventually finding a café that's open and sit down inside while the rain beats against the windows. You look like a complete fool with the plasters across your nose. But it makes no difference here. And why should the two of you go back? What's stopping you from staying? What is there back home that the two of you couldn't do without? Who exactly wouldn't it be a relief to get rid of? Anything at all, if Amalie wants it. *Anywhere in the world,* as long as Amalie comes along.

"Do you not even regret it?" you ask her.

"What should I regret?"

"That he was your first?"

"What difference does it make? Would it have been better if it had been someone else?"

You stand there with your mouth open wide, speechless at how inconsiderate she's being, her insensitivity, the complete absence of a loving perspective in what she just said, as though she didn't care a jot, as if nothing she said had any real meaning, as if she doesn't have a clue what real love is.

"So it wouldn't have meant anything to you, then," you finally manage to stammer, "if it had been me the first time?"

"Okay," she says (but only because you compelled her): "So it would have been nice. But it didn't turn out that way. Surely the most important thing is how things are between us now?"

"But don't you even wish that it had been the two of us the first time? That it had been the first time for both of us?"

"Yes. Of course. But it didn't turn out that way. Is it really such a big deal?"

"Is it such a big deal?" you mimic, in utter disbelief again at the indifference of your sweetheart, who obviously could have had it off with whoever and been just as happy, no matter what. You picture how it would be if you were gone somewhere for a while, how even after a relatively short time it would become uncontrollable, how she wouldn't be able to restrain herself, how already on the second or third day she would cast all inhibitions and throw herself into the waiting orgies that are always there, that want her along at all times, that are a standing offer, that tempt and entice and will get their way if you are the tiniest bit inattentive for a little too long. You ask if that's the way she wants it, if that's what she's thirsty for, if that's what she's going around waiting for an opportunity to slip off and abandon herself to, if that's her dream, if that's what she fantasizes about every hour of the day. You tell her that if that's what she wants then go ahead, fire away, you won't be the one to stand in her way. There are enough horndogs out there, she can probably pick and choose. Or if she fancies going back to Doberman and picking up where she left off, then she can hop on the first train and go: one phone call from her and he'll be ready no doubt. Because it's nothing, is it, what you give her, compared with what he gave her, and can give her, if she gives him another chance? That was the dream fuck, wasn't it? Nothing else has ever come close. Never going to see the likes of that again. There'll never be anyone who can measure up to the one who took her virginity, the one who had her when she was still fresh and green and up for anything, the one who could do as he fancied, instruct her in whatever perversities he wished. The man in leather. The beast. Gorgeous Mr. Horny. The fucker she can't forget.

She's sitting opposite you in the café in town, yellow coat on, her hair up, you've been to the movies and are both feeling dejected, your parents have forbidden her to spend the night at your place, and you aren't allowed to go home with her, that's part of the punishment they've given you after the Copenhagen trip, she's getting the last bus and it leaves in half an hour. Suddenly she brightens up and says: "Shall we go to the Seychelles?"

"What? Tonight, you mean?"

"No, not tonight, you twit. When we're finished with school. If we save up the money."

"The Seychelles . . . Why do you want to go there?"

"Because they're supposed to be the most beautiful islands in the world."

She looks at you as though to check if it's a good enough reason.

"Plus it's such a nice name," she continues. "So pleasant to say."

"The Seychelles?" you say and feel the lump in your throat thicken again, without you knowing why.

"The Seychelles," she says.

"It's settled then," you say, your throat so swollen that your voice is distorted, "We'll go to the Seychelles."

You walk her to the bus stop, there's nobody else there, and for a little while you're hoping the bus has gone, that she's missed it and that she'll have to stay over at your house all the same. You stand against one another, you with your head resting on her shoulder, her humming as usual, the sound vibrating in your temple. She received a letter from the university earlier today to inform her she'd been accepted on the course she'd applied for, which meant moving in the autumn, lots of practical things to sort out, your sister knows someone who's the super at a student-run block of bedsits and has promised to get the two of you to the front of the queue. Then the bus comes, she tears herself away and gets on, you standing looking after her, a yellow figure walking down the aisle reaching out for every second seat on each side, the bus pulling out and accelerating away, and for a moment the movements offset one another, the bus going forward, her going backward, for a few seconds the distance between the two of you is the same, even though in reality she's moving away from you at speed.

In the spring there's the endless round of pre-graduation parties and drinking. Every guy you know has suddenly been transformed into a party animal and a hell-raiser, even the most timid, all letting loose the same way, all as horny as each other. And Amalie, if she could do it with Doberman then couldn't she do it with anyone? You want to go along with it all, get carried away, together with Amalie, you want to grow dizzy again, together with her, dance until you collapse. You want to be part of the society of the living. You have been and you want to be again, you want resumption, you want to join in anew, be rapt anew, forget everything, nothing within you but the moment, throw what was and what will be overboard, just be, just do, just love. But there's a lump stuck in your throat, you can't swallow without feeling it, it's like a plastic tube that's been forced down your gullet. You see Amalie, her head to the side, smiling, radiant, prettier than ever, and something churns inside you, everything good changes course and sticks in your throat as something bad, everything you experience puts you in mind of something terrible, every single pleasure contains fear, fear wrapped up in pleasure: pleasure is the wrapping paper, fear the only thing you actually feel.

She's going along to a meet of all the high school seniors in the country. You can't go because of your father's sixtieth birthday. Right up until the end you're hoping she'll change her mind and stay home, right up until the day the gathering is happening you walk around waiting for the call from her to say she's not going after all, that since you're not going she couldn't be bothered either. But the call never comes. And finally the day arrives, the dreaded date, the terrible hour, which confirms once and for all that there was never any doubt in her mind as to what she wanted, that there was never any question of her doing anything other than indulging herself, dancing, drinking, necking, groping and being groped. In the evening, after the birthday party, you throw up, filling the toilet bowl with a sweet porridge of cakes and soda, and for the rest of the night you stand in the wings watching her, following her with your eyes while she dances with one guy after the other, arms around their necks, rubbing up against them, letting them feel her up, cavorting, helping herself greedily to all that is offered her, while you stand the whole time watching, not one look, not one touch, not one sweet word escapes your attention, you lie staring up at the ceiling until it's bright outside, watching it all unfold minute for minute, hour for hour, how she, free from the weight of you, is so happy to join the dance, how she takes the world by storm, how she does with everyone what she wants them to do with her, how they take her with them to the toilet, every guy that's there, taking turns to screw her in the cubicle. The sun comes up, shining on everything, revealing everything, showing you everything as it really is, showing you the toilet at the disco in town, where Amalie spreads herself for the seventeenth or eighteenth in succession.

Okay, so you're jealous! But what else can you be? Anyone who's never been jealous has probably never been in love. Anyone who's never been subjected to the madness of jealousy, has probably never been loved. Jealousy is the same as love. Jealousy is exaggerated love. What's love worth, if it isn't exaggerated? What does a person feel if they never feel jealous? If you aren't jealous then what in the world are you?

Then, all at once, you're happy again. It's summer, you're off traveling, just the two of you, and in your overblown, lovesick mind you're the first people to set foot wherever you alight from the train, wherever you decide to unroll your sleeping bags, you can imagine how upon your return you can proudly unfold history's first fully drawn map of each and every European country and city. Everything is new, freshly discovered, innocent, nothing's weighing you down, you're both free from everything and are able to start afresh every day. You're strong, unbreakable steel reinforced and ready for anything, ready for more than anything, you can hardly wait, you're aching to try out your invincible powers on something, just like one of those old Japanese warriors someone told you about, so impatient to try out a new sword that they chopped the head off the first person they met.

As if that's not enough you begin to write, thoughts, diary entries, reflections, the strangest ideas, some of which even resemble poems, in a red and black exercise book Amalie bought you before you left and said you should use to write down the story of what she had already dubbed "The European Adventure." You'd looked at her at first, not thinking you could. But from the moment you opened it and tried out the pen that came with it, the sentences have flowed over the pages, as though the ability to write was also a part of the gift: the words have followed one another without stop, as though you could write all the time if you so wished, as though Amalie had opened the door to yet another room within you, a room full of things, as it turned out, unused things, things you didn't know you owned, enough for weeks, months, years, enough for hundreds and thousands of pages, enough for a whole string of books.

"Are you a poet, then?" she asks, conquering your heart for the thousandth time.

Then she breaks out laughing and strokes you across the cheek.

"I knew it! You are a poet!"

That night you write: *I stand in the pet's open space listening to the reverb. I imbibe brick buildings that burn my tongue. I capture you with gun and net and show you the one eye, because we are butterflies in fantastic colors.*

A faint shimmer from the carriage you're in sweeps over the ditches along the railroad track. The fields outside are sometimes yellow and other times red. Gray silos and brown chimneys rise up here and there. The two of you drink cheap German wine. The train pulls its load faster and faster through the naked landscape. Everything rattles. And you feel how the same velocity is to be found within you, that you're also hurtling into the sharp turns like a furious buffalo. You're one with the vehicles on the track, with the stampeding carriages. It can't go fast enough. And you revel in it. You know you can write a poem a day for the rest of your life. You tear through towns, a whole host of towns, where the lights flash and change place. Wires run along right in front of your eyes, rising, falling, rising. You have a squid in your head squirting black ink, more and more of home is blotted out the further from it you both travel. Forget everything, you think. Turn your back, put it behind you, rush away, flee without thinking. Memory is a chain. To remember is to tether yourself. To forget is to set yourself free. At one spot there's a fire, a barn is ablaze, a few cows stand in a field nearby looking at it while nodding their heads.

But a shadow darkens The European Adventure, a shadow follows you everywhere, a shadow leans over Amalie together with your own: Doberman's shadow: it chases you like a specter throughout Europe. Turning up everywhere, even in the smallest village on the Costa del Sol it finds you, even in your happiest moments it sneaks up on you. You stand in front of her undressing and you think: *this is how he took his clothes off for her, while she lay on the sofa waiting* . . . You enter her gently and you think: *this is how he guided his cock into her* . . . She moans and you think: *this is how she lay groaning while he banged away at her* . . . She wriggles free, bends down and takes you in her mouth and you think . . . *This is how she knelt in front of him and opened wide* . . . You begin to come, you stand looking at her while you're coming and you think: *this is how she knelt, only she was more randy then, and let him blow his load in her face* . . . Everything you do with Amalie is a repetition of what Doberman has done with her. Everything the two of you experience together has its loathsome duplicate in the thought of what the two of them have already done.

Amalie is a vampire and you're an Indian, and before you know it you're being crushed in the throng of witches, pirates, clowns, pixies, monsters, and gorillas, an undulating sea of masks, Amalie somewhere in the crowd, you see her emerge from under it, then she's pulled back down, she pops up again, then she's pulled back down, without it seeming to bother her, the fact that you're getting further and further away from one another, or that she can't see you and doesn't know where you are at all times. You're conscious of people talking to you, but you don't listen, you don't answer them, you're too busy looking around for Amalie, the black collar, the white face, the crimson mouth (which caused you a sudden pang as you were both making yourselves up, when you saw how good she looked, you who had thought she was going to end up looking like a monster). You look this way and that, but can't catch sight of her anywhere. She's there but you've no idea where. You make your way through the crowd, glancing all around, think you've found her, but it turns out to be someone else. There are several vampires there, their costumes resemble hers. Was it planned? Is she getting some of the others to dress up like her, to make it easier for her to slip away? Strobes are flashing. The commotion all around is clipped into frames. Then you see her: she's standing at the back bar talking to a gorilla. Suddenly her head is thrown back in laughter. Suddenly she's leaning forward. Suddenly her arm is around him. Suddenly they're necking. Suddenly she's rubbing his crotch.

Finally you reach them. Amalie pulling away, you notice, as soon as she spots you. The gorilla casts a glance at you. You can see through the eyeholes that he's drunk. You pull the mask off him. But you don't know him, you've never seen him before.

And when you turn to Amalie, she's gone. The gorilla shouts something at you. You give him back the mask and set off in the direction Amalie disappeared in. The muffled rhythm of the bass thumps in your stomach while again you force your way through the crowd, which is like a maelstrom, an interminable swirling, a vice being tightened and tightened. Right until you catch sight of her again. And then the vice tightens even more, because now she's on the dance floor, writhing and wiggling in rapture. There's a guy in a police uniform, equally entranced, banging his pelvis against her while she just stands there gyrating with eyes closed, letting him grind into her as much as he wants, as if there was nothing she liked more. You try to make it over to her, but the crush is too strong, you're pressed back each time you make any headway. Eventually you succeed in working your way through the people dancing, but from a different side, and when you've wriggled your way between all the others, over to the spot where she was standing, she's gone. Where can they have got to? You crane to look. No Amalie. Lots of vampires, but none of them her. You suddenly notice a door, right down the back, being opened. Two heads disappearing behind it, one of them Amalie, the other a policeman. With your heart pounding, you begin a new expedition through the throng, being bumped and jostled into new detours all the time, but finally you make it to the door, and without daring to consider what sight awaits you beyond, you tug it open and enter a long dark corridor with people standing along the whole length of one wall. They all peer at you, as though you'd fallen from the sky. It takes your brain a while to register that the queue is composed solely of girls. They laugh at you. None of them is Amalie. And none of them are wearing a police uniform. So where have they got to, the two you saw coming in? Are there more doors? More rooms further along? Secret alcoves? Little pleasure booths known only to a select few? Finally you give up and head back into the disco. The pounding of the music is formidable, it feels like your heart has tumbled down into your stomach. You're on your way to the exit to start searching for her all over again when you sense her, more than see her, to the right of you. You turn. She's standing with her back to you, leaning over a table where two guys are sitting. It looks like she's tonguing both of them at the same time. When you make it over, you realize someone's hand is in Amalie's hair. And it doesn't look like she minds in the slightest, being held like that. You take hold of her arm and spin her around. The movement takes her by surprise and she loses her balance and falls. You can't manage to catch her. Suddenly she's lying on the floor. The guys at the table get to their feet. One of them gets between you and Amalie. You shove him aside and bend down to help her. But someone else gets there ahead of you. A hand helps her to her feet. She stands there looking at you. The others gather around you both. Glances are exchanged. You reach out to her. She pushes your hand away. And in a pyramid of glass hanging just below the ceiling you catch sight of yourself, in the middle of the crowd. You look like a ten-year-old in those beige suede pants, that beige waistcoat with the tassels, that stupid headband, with those wispy feathers sticking up from it at all angles, a figure of ridicule, the moron at the party, the guy everyone will talk about the next day.

On the way home she screams at you, stands in the middle of the street, her hands to her head screaming that she can't take it anymore, that she's going to go crazy if this keeps up, the mascara running from her eyes, black lines branching out over her cadaverous makeup, you hold her, try to calm her down and she collapses in your arms, nothing holding her up any longer, as though her skeleton is melting, and then you fall down, both of you, people pass and stare but no one stops, no one gets involved. "What kind of person do you take me for?" she sobs. "What kind of fucking person do you take me for?" She mumbles something else, which you don't catch, and sits there rocking back and forth as if she's riding a horse. You have pains in your stomach, they're spreading out to the rest of your body and up to your head, your brain feels like it's made of metal, harder than the skull it's stored in. Then she falls asleep. You hold her tight. The closed shops resemble dreaming faces, and the asphalt is freezing, the cold going right through your stupid suede pants, you shudder all over, sit shivering while you hold her tight, and she's shaking too, lying there shaking and snoring at the same time, and as the two of you sit like that, and the shuddering gradually subsides, you dictate your next letter to her: *My Darling Amalie, I'll get it together. I swear. Anything for you. Anything for us. That was the last time, I swear. I don't know what's going on. I don't know why I act like that. Can you forgive me? I take back everything I said. I didn't mean it. You must know that, that I would never mean it? But that was the last time. Never again. Never again. Just promise me you'll never leave me and I'll never, ever act like that again.*

Fried Egg on a Plate without the Plate

You don't know what she's called, you don't know where she's from, you don't know what her voice sounds like, you have no basis for making any assumptions about her character, her personality, yet you know, the moment you see her, that with her, *with her you will finally experience happiness.* Because there's no doubt: the two of you are going to be together. Not tomorrow. Not next week either. Not in a year, for that matter. But some time. Some day. When the time comes. The two of you are going to be together.

A whole year passes. You look at her, every single chance you get. You: obsessed with the sight of her. Her: still unaware of your existence. You don't lose heart, not even when you see her together more and more often with one of the boys from the year above. You're just as calm, just as patient and just as assured. You know that nothing can come in the way of what's already been decided. You see them running down the street, weaving in and out of cars honking their horns, hand in hand, while they yell and scream, and you think: Have a good time while you can, Lucky Jim, enjoy it while it lasts. Her boyfriend is almost twice her size, covered in hair, on his face, on his hands, on his neck, probably all over the rest of his body too, he looks like a bear, a huge grizzly bear, and this makes you admire her all the more, that she fell for him and not one of the smooth, good-looking types who rule the schoolyard and can get any girl they like, no matter how pretty.

As though in a fairy tale, as though the fulfilment of some fanciful dream, you come back after summer, having had a girlfriend for the two weeks you were on holidays with your parents, and you're suddenly sitting beside her, in the third row of what is now, due to you both picking the same subjects, your new class. Already by the first break you turn to her, without thinking what you're doing. "Good seats!" you hear yourself say, in almost a cheeky tone of voice and rap your knuckles on the desk several times, without having any idea why, so stunned by yourself you nearly want to run out of the room. She blushes. And you find you haven't got a clue of what else to say, that the sentence you just uttered was the last one you had. Is this what they mean by "your mind going blank"? What on earth do you say to a girl after having declared that they certainly were good seats you both got?

Then the miracle takes place. The girl says something back, something that's no problem finding an acceptable answer to. And then it just pours out of you, one thing after the other. The conversation takes care of itself. And while you're talking, you suddenly see her name, written in big, decorative letters, which are shaded, on the cover of a book, this name, you realize, you've never taken the trouble to find out, limiting yourself solely as you have to waiting and observing (as if you knew it would all come in good time: her name, her voice, her eyes, her hands, her lips). She's wearing a purple trouser suit, sitting on top of the desk eating a yoghurt, without a spoon, she's partly guzzling it, partly licking it, in the most deft fashion, without spilling a drop. Her eyes are round and dark brown, and now they're looking at you, now they're fixed on you, now she's talking to you, that slightly husky voice of hers is directed toward you, the two of you are having a conversation, she's showing an interest in what you have to say, she's even close to laughing a few times, and she's not only listening and answering, but telling you things too, bringing up one thing after another herself, and asking questions, if you say something unclear or if you need to elaborate further.

That something so beautiful on the surface could conceal something so beautiful on the inside is beyond you. She's pretty *and* nice. She's stunning to look at *and* pleasant to talk to. No, it's not possible. It can't be true! But it is possible. It is true. She's sitting right there, straight in front of you. She's talking to you. She's looking at you. Her eyes rest upon you. A revolution has taken place. The Law of The Inverse Relation is rescinded. The prettiest girl is also the nicest!

You continue the conversation at the next break. And there's nothing about her to suggest she doesn't like it, that she'd rather be talking to someone else, that you're detaining her, taking up valuable time, keeping her from doing something else. No, it seems like something she wants to do. It seems she's given it first priority, just like that. That for the present moment you top the list of preferred conversational partners. If anybody else in the class had come over and butted in you would have hit them.

You chat together until the bell rings. About everything under the sun. She doesn't laugh because something is embarrassing or because she's not taking what you say seriously enough. She treats everything just as seriously. She only laughs when something is supposed to be humorous. She laughs when you tell her about something funny that's happened. And listens soberly when you tell her something serious. She has a little skeleton in an army uniform on her bag that rattles when she puts it on her back. And on the cover of her history book she's written a quote by Andy Warhol, something about McDonald's being the most beautiful thing in all the cities of the world, except for Peking and Moscow, which don't have anything beautiful yet.

At lunch break you're out in the schoolyard, her with some friends, you with some mates. And suddenly you catch sight of him, the hairy bear, over by the covered bike rack standing looking out over the crowd. For what? For her. And perhaps he locates her, all at once he seems to fix his gaze. He looks like a wounded animal, a sad bear, towering head and shoulders above everyone else around him.

You turn in the direction the bear is staring, and sure enough, there, at the other end of the yard, she stands, in the middle of a group of girls, just like you saw her exactly a year ago. And now it's as though you know her. It's as though you're already together, have been for a long time and you know everything about one another. Then she laughs, and now you recognize her voice in the rippling laughter. And you can picture it, how the two of you will soon dash through the city streets, yelling and screaming, hand in hand, dodging in and out between fuming motorists. And then she turns and makes eye contact, and before you have time to think you've smiled to her, and now she smiles back, holding your gaze a little with an expression which you interpret as meaning she'd rather be standing over there, together with you, before turning back to her friends (one of which, it looks like, has registered the eye contact and leans over to whisper something to one of the others).

A week later you're sitting in the dark on a veranda holding one another tight and telling each other about your families, how many brothers and sisters you have and what your parents work at. Behind you the music is pounding, and in front of you black water is lapping at an invisible beach. The hours fly by, but you keep yourselves warm. Now and then someone staggers past, but nobody discovers the two of you, they just piss or throw up and disappear again. Beyond the dark water of the lake, you can see the lights of the town, resembling a starry sky. You both sit motionless for hours. You hold around her and think: Now I'm never going to feel frightened, dissatisfied or bored again. You think: Everything that happens to me from now on will be meaningful. Everything I go through, I'll go through in order to be better able to take care of you. Only my best will be good enough. By your side, Amalie, my courage is boundless.

She's standing at the large window in the living room, it's the first time she's been in your house, winter's arrived during the night, snow covering the garden, clumps hanging from the tree-tops, and you have an hour to yourselves before your parents get home. She's got that solemn, attentive expression, listening out for something far away. You're behind her, she has a curve at the base of her back that's all her own, that would help you pick her out no matter how far away she was, all her weight resting on one leg, making her backside jut into an elegant arc. You walk over and press up against her, she brings her arms around behind her and locks you in. A flock of birds take flight from a single tree and disappear into the sky like a mini armada. You don't know which you think would be best: if no one else was in love with her, or if everybody was.

Her father is an artist, her mother an architect. Their house looks like a sanatorium, situated on a slope north of town. It's an old wooden house that has stood there for years, Amalie's informed you, and now features an enormous glass and concrete extension. She's waiting for you at the bus stop when you arrive, you're wearing a shirt you haven't worn since your confirmation. You've been dreading having to meet her parents for a long time. Nobody turns up to welcome you as you enter, but loud music can be heard from one of the rooms, an orchestra playing wildly, drums and timpani booming. You step over a raised threshold, worn down to a U-shape in the middle, indicating the transition from the old part of the house to the new. There are piles of papers and stacks of books all over the place, things lying thrown about, a pungent smell coming from somewhere, and in the living room, beside the fireplace there's a sculpture with a colossal member sticking up into the air.

"Do you want to say hello to Dad?" asks Amalie. You really feel like saying no but you nod, and she takes you by the hand and leads you up a narrow staircase to the second floor. The smell increases in strength. She opens a door. You enter a huge room, light flooding down from the ceiling, which is made of glass. There's stuff everywhere in here as well, on the walls, along the shelves, on tables and stools and over the floor. At the far end of the room there's a man standing in a black gown with his back to you, painting something that looks like a cross between Dracula and Donald Duck. He stands there for a good while before he turns around.

"Now." He says. "What do you think?"

When neither of you reply, he snorts and gives his daughter a despairing look.

"Just so you know, Amalie, I'm really not ready for any grandchildren just yet!" he calls out, shaking his brushes in our direction, before turning back to the canvas and beginning to paint again.

Her mother is waiting for you down in the kitchen, she takes you by the hand, you say hello and then you sit down at the table, all three of you. Now and again in the course of the conversation her mother addresses you, but the answers you give are, you get the feeling, a disappointment, each one greater than the next. And you can hear how lively the conversation is and how freely it flows as soon as they're the only ones talking. What have you got to contribute, seeing as they know everything and don't have any respect for anything? The only thing you dare to say, after having sat and fine-tuned the sentence inside you, is to ask her mother what kind of music it was she was playing when the two of you came in.

"*The Rite of Spring*," she says. "Did you like it?"

The question is so abrupt that you don't manage to answer one way or the other, both would be just as dumb, so you just grin. Her mother looks at you with incredulity, as if she's never come across such a twerp. And gradually you drop out of the conversation. You feel like a civil servant, sitting there in the white shirt your mum's ironed for you. Then her mother gets up, says it's been nice meeting you but that she has to get back to work. When she's left, Amalie smiles and tells you she loves you. The boom of timpani comes from the study. "*The Rite of Spring*," you think, what kind of name is that for music?

When you get home that night your parents' place seems empty. It's like there's nobody living there. It's neat and tidy everywhere, the same meticulous order prevails throughout, not one thing is out of place. You walk into the living room and stand looking around in amazement. The house seems uninhabited. It's like a museum. It's like nothing happens there. As though nobody lives there. As though not one trace of human activity is to be found anywhere.

Amalie shows no signs of concern at the reception her family gave you, the next day in school she doesn't mention it at all. But the eccentric behavior of her parents is something she's no doubt well used to, you think. And the fact that it doesn't bother her, nor does she pretend it does, makes her all the more adorable, all the more special in your eyes, as though she were somehow apart, just as though she belonged in a superior, wonderful world, where even trivial, everyday things have the luster of something mystical, something spiritual. You think about the shimmer that surrounds her when you see her together with the others at school, how she shines among her friends in the class, now you know where it comes from, that light, and you admire her all the more, her and this world she belongs in, and you're all the more overwhelmed by her matter-of-course attitude to things which in her world are common and which in yours would have provoked gossip, indignation and contempt.

You're over at her place, a whole gang of you from school, when her father comes barging into her room, his eyes wild. "Make some noise!" he roars, spit flying: "Create a commotion! Shout! Sing! Dance!" You all sit in stunned silence, no one daring to move. "Smash the TV!" he continues. "Throw the furniture out the window! Fill the house with screams and yells! What the hell is the point of being young if you're going to just sit there drinking tea as if you were a bunch of senile old paragons?!"

You're asked if you want to stay for dinner, an invitation held in high regard judging by the reaction of the others: fortunately they haven't left when her mother puts her head around the door to ask. Twice you have to call home and tell them you'll be late, because the food isn't on the table before nine o'clock! A big cast-iron casserole filled with cooked vegetables is placed in the middle of the table. Some bread beside it, that's it, you sit waiting for the main course when you see Amalie has already begun dishing it out on her plate. Midway through the meal her father arrives, he sits down and helps himself greedily, but talks more than he eats, his mouth moving a mile a minute, before he stands up abruptly and leaves. You look at Amalie, but she just smiles and mouths a question, if you like the food? Her mother sits, sticking her fork on the plate, more in hope of piercing something on the prongs than aiming, while reading a magazine. Are they always like this, you wonder, or is it being put on for my benefit, in order to embarrass me, to test me, to see how long I hold out?

But that's the way they do things. They do what suits them.

Compared with what you're used to, everything is turned on its head. Chaos reigns. Do what you like is the only law. At the same time you see how naturally it comes to them, how they do it without a thought, all busy at any given time with their own thing, sometimes intersecting one another, sometimes gathered, if circumstances permit, free to choose what they want, free to get up and go whenever they want and free to leave most of the food on their plate. Yes, you can see what a lovely world it is and the ease with which they move around within it. And you think about everything you've grown up with as the right way, the only correct way for a family to be: you didn't know it was possible to live any other way. Now you see how replaceable it is, all of it. Everything that you've known up until now as being the only right way, *always conform, always do something other than what you'd rather, always delay what appeals to you most, always leave the best until last, always eat fish before eating spaghetti*, it suddenly hits you that it doesn't need to be like that, you suddenly realize that it's okay to reject things and replace them with something else.

Even after you've long been accepted as part of the family—*I'm their future son-in-law!* you think: *I'm the one who's going to marry their only daughter!*—you still get the same feeling from her parents, of them making fun of you, that deep down they shudder at how ordinary you are. It's as though there's an undertone of derision in everything they say and all they ask you about. But you don't take it to heart. You're willing to be walked on and ridiculed, you're happy to suffer the barbs: it's a challenge, a struggle you have to wage in order to win Amalie, a barrier you have to break through in order to prove yourself worthy, a transformation you have to undergo in order to come up to her—their—level. You're serving an apprenticeship, an apprenticeship which involves systematically razing everything to the ground so as to build it up again, to prepare you to face the new world, *the real world.*

And this education, this transformation, is in the end the only thing that interests you. From now on the sole value of things is dependent on how exotic they appear. Everything familiar has an air of lifelessness about it, which you're only able to view with forbearance. Your parents are more removed to you than ever. They're like an extinct race. All you hail from, your whole background, your history, turns plain in the light from *her*, from *them.* For the first time you see yourself through other eyes than your own. And what you see makes you feel ashamed.

Sometimes, if her father's in the mood, you're allowed into the atelier while he paints. You like the smell in there, the unwholesome feeling, the dark, corrupted, poisonous atmosphere: it can't possibly be healthy to draw a breath in there, and you love it. And you like to hear his brushes against the canvas, the quick repeated rubbing, and the resulting sound, as from a drum, against the stretched fabric. And you consider, almost with a feeling of alarm, the incredible fact that the man standing there in the floor-length gown, covered in flecks of paint in all the colors of the rainbow, he who has knowingly created this chaos about him, he for whom this mad world is his everyday life, for whom this strange place and all these strange things are *work*, are *an occupation*, that this man is the same age as your father! And you peer around the fantastic clutter of his atelier, which looks like the contents of an overturned truck from a circus of oddities and rarities, and think about the punctilious regime at home in Nordseterveien, the shelves with nicely lined up ornaments, brittle as the fingers of little old ladies. You study the pictures and sketches hanging on the walls, you leaf through the books lying around in piles on the floor, you pick up some of the strange objects, masks, bones, figures, tools, and every time you do, almost without fail, you suddenly hear his voice from over at the easel, relating a few short facts to explain what it is, the item you have in your hand, and where it originates from, as if he had eyes in the back of his head or a sixth sense. And usually there's more, bearing no relation to what the two of you have talked about previously or anything you've asked about, as though he were thinking out loud while working. What he's going on about is not necessarily meant for you, nor is it important for you to comprehend it, but you're more than welcome to try, if you want, to understand these sentences you can't make head nor tail of, not before you've thought about them for a long time. It's as though he speaks to you in riddles, and you, the apprentice, are left with the task of solving them. But then, when you first understand, you understand everything, then you see the truth in what her father has said, then you see how incontrovertible his strange opinions are, his obscure assertions about the difference between men and women, the relationship between art and reality, or the correlation between sex and the creative process, things like that, things you've never heard anyone talk about, things you didn't have the foggiest clue about, and no interest in either, but which now in the magical, turpentine-scented light of Amalie's father's atelier, you realize belong to the most important, most fundamental aspects of life. It's a new way of looking at the world, a new sense of you and of everything around you, of yourself as part of the cosmos, of your own place in all this, yes, because you're a part of it too, you're also marked on the map being unfolded for you, this vast network of context and meaning, this infinite universe which has been closed and concealed, but which now has finally begun to open up to you.

You think: Why has nobody told me this before? Why on earth has nobody told me this before?

You're standing with your feet apart in a snowdrift, the moon hanging clear and bright above the edge of the forest in front of you, so close you can count the lines and stick your finger in every crater. The urine drums upon the icy crust, you direct the jet as well as you can: if anyone saw you they'd think you were dancing. Afterwards you stand admiring your handiwork and wishing she were there to see it. *Amalie,* it says, in steaming cursive script; it looks like someone has written with corrosive ink on a sheet of blue paper sprinkled with glitter.

You and Amalie are allowed along to a costume party her parents are throwing, with a number of her father's colleagues in attendance as well as lots of other people from town whom you've never seen before, who you had no idea lived there and whom you're amazed you've never noticed; one of them struts around naked all night, "dressed up as Adam." Amalie has painted a yellow bolt of lightning across her face, while you have a gray cloud on your forehead and large raindrops on both cheeks.

It's as though everything is underwater and you and Amalie are the only people equipped with gills. Amalie's mother is sitting with her arms around a woman the whole night, they send one another lustful looks, kiss one another on the mouth a few times, and you see them use their tongues at least once. And when you're on your way to the toilet, late at night, Amalie's father comes out of one of the bedrooms hand in hand with a girl, and they both snigger when they see you, snigger like drunken teenagers in love.

It goes against everything within you, what you see, and you find it alluring, since they're the ones doing it, your new guides in life; you find it alluring because it goes against everything within you, like you were viewing it through a wall which was solid before but is now full of cracks and holes, and it's only a question of time before it comes crashing down.

"Look at them!" cries her father, pointing at Amalie and her mother.

You daren't look at them nor at her father.

"Look at them! They're women! They should count themselves lucky! Men are good for nothing! We just ruin our lives! Woman is the true human being! We're merely a subspecies! Since we can't take the world out of our stomachs, we try to take it out of our heads! Woman lives, man paints.

You talk all the time. There's always one of you with something on their mind. It doesn't matter what it is, every word she articulates shows some new side of her, tells you something about her you didn't know before. You feel a tingle every time you realize she's going to say something, you're hardly able to wait. And while the two of you sit at your parents' house holding each other's hands, responding politely to their questions about school, further education and your plans for the future, back at her house you live a dissolute life where anything goes, where obstacles and restrictions no longer exist, every day is a party, a celebration.

The sun is going down as you reach the top. You had to ski the last part in a single-poling skate, Amalie in tow; she's been whining like a baby the whole way, sitting down on her ass in the snow at one stage and refusing to get up. But now you're finally at the top, the landscape stretching out, the sky looking like Salvador Dalí painted it, two vapor trails from intersecting planes, and high above you can both see the peaks of the Rondane and the Jotunheimen, and far below lies the town, hidden behind sloping ridges.

Now she's smiling again, her hair sticking out from under the hood of the anorak gray with frost like a spiderweb, and suddenly you know what she'll look like when she's old, and you picture it, the next time you're up here, and how you'll have one or two others along with you then, calling you mummy and daddy.

The two of you go over to the round metal board erected by the tourist council, which has an arrow you can move around to point at the names of all the mountains you can see. Amalie is indescribably cute in the old-fashioned ski gear she's wearing, like a postcard from the 1950s. You let your gaze wander the whole way around the melting Dalí horizon. You think: I can see the curvature of the earth from here.

*Dear A*
*If I were the wind, a soft breeze would always caress you . . .*
*If I were the sea, I would carry you alone upon my waves . . .*
*If I were the earth, I would kiss your feet . . .*
*If I were the rain, I would wash your face . . .*
*If I were the sun, a ray would always fall upon your forehead . . .*
*If I were your shadow, I would never leave you . . .*
*If I were your shadow, I would not be able to leave you . . .*
*I am your shadow, I can never leave you . . .*

You don't see him until he's right alongside you and it seems like he can't bring himself to pass you by and continue on his own, not before he's said something. You recall the nervous young teacher who called the two of you Siamese twins, and Stein-Ove who whistled "Here Comes the Bride" every time the two of you entered the classroom. It's like lifting the lid off a box of memories. The town in the clear early morning light, reminiscent of a knight who's fallen asleep in his armor. The squeaking of the wheelwork turning the gigantic pack of butter round and round up on the corner of the roof on the margarine factory. The huge dark barrel at the entrance to the outdoor restaurant on the far side of the waterfall. All this which belonged to the two of you and which you could do what you wanted with, transform into anything, the Planet of the Apes, the red deserts of Mars, the city walls of Karanthor, the corpses, like blood-stained pin cushions, which the sun shone upon.

You traipse alongside one another a while. Anybody looking would think you were together. You wait for him to say something, to make some remark about you and Amalie. But he doesn't open his mouth, not before the school clock tower comes into view.

"How's it going?" he asks, without turning his head.

"Great," you reply, surprised by the meekness in his voice. "Excellent!" You add, as if to rub it in. For the second time in your life you're bigger than Oskar Wang. And this time you just enjoy it. You enjoy it to the full, without any qualms, you claim it as a right, as an opportune installment, for insult and injury caused, as it were.

"And you?" you ask in return.

"Good," replies Oskar, but again there's something lifeless in his voice, as though he wants you to see through his lie. You steal a glance and make out how utterly dejected he looks, like he'd begin to cry if anyone touched him, as if all that's left of your best friend, who became your tormentor, is a frail shell holding neither of them, a listless wimp wandering around in the world, with neither friend nor victim to lead him the right way.

You cross the parking lot together, but the bustle of the schoolyard soon pulls you your separate ways. You start to look around for Amalie. You think about how no matter what Oskar could have thought of saying to you that you wouldn't have let it hurt you. Nothing can bring you down. Nothing can force you to your knees. As long as nothing comes between you and Amalie, then anything at all can come between the two of you and the rest of the world, it wouldn't matter, it still wouldn't make any difference this way or that. You both have what you need. You're self-sufficient. You're immune. The two of you would survive any war, disaster or epidemic you faced.

Then you glimpse something yellow, over by the bike racks. You begin to make your way over. You can't wait until you reach her, until she catches sight of you and beams at you, until she laughs and stretches her arms out toward you, until she tilts her head to the side and kisses you.

You're suddenly aware of a smell, a pungent odor, from some-where or another. You inhale slowly through your nose. Genitals. It smells of genitals. And it's coming from you. It's coming from your mouth, your mouth smells of genitals. Your chin, your lips, your teeth, they all reek of Amalie's genitals. You take a peek at your parents, who haven't noticed anything, sitting concentrat-ing on their dinner, both of them. Then there's an almighty waft, which couldn't possibly escape their attention. It's as though you're sitting with a twat where your mouth should be. You're expecting the first comment any second. It's only a question of time. You picture your father, putting down his knife and fork, sniffing at the air and asking: "What's that smell?" And you press your lips together, sit for the remainder of the meal picking at your food, knowing that under no circumstances are you going to be able to put any more into your mouth.

Aksel and Amalie. Aksel and Amalie. You hear it when others say it, the rhythm it has, how natural it sounds. Aksel and Amalie. Like a physical constant. Something no power in the world can separate. Amalie = forty-one, Aksel = forty-eight. Put them together and you get eighty-nine. If you add those two digits together you get seventeen. Add one and seven and you get eight. Put eight on its side and it's the symbol for infinity. You pick up the phone to ring and tell her, but as you lift the receiver and are about to put in her number you hear her voice: "Hello? Aksel?"

As if in a dream: there she is.

As you and Bente are eating supper you tell her what happened.

"Unbelievable, huh?" you say.

But she just rolls her eyes: "So what?"

"So what? Come on, it's incredible! At the very moment that she's finished putting in our number, I pick up the phone to call her!"

Bente belches, takes her glass and plate and stands up.

"The amount the two of you ring each other it's a miracle it hasn't happened before."

On her way out of the kitchen she adds: "Should be fun to hear what Dad says when the telephone bill arrives."

Late one night there's a program about surrealism on TV. Fortunately the others have gone to bed, so you're at liberty to enjoy it free from ironic remarks. But just as Dalí is dancing around the beach in Port Lligat with a sea urchin on his head, you catch a whiff of Bente's pimple cream and hear her garbled voice behind you: "What the fuck is with that guy?"

You try to ignore her, but to your annoyance she remains standing behind your chair, her and her stink, and all of a sudden there's nothing left of the genius on the screen in front of you other than a downright nutcase. Bente swears, as well as she can through a mouthful of toothpaste foam, runs the brush across her teeth a couple more times, then takes it out with a slurp and swears again.

"Fucking hell, how crazy is that guy?"

Eventually you've had enough and, switching off the TV in the middle of a clip from *Un Chien Andalou*, you get up and stand shaking the remote control at her, so enraged you're almost stammering as you try to explain to your imbecile of a sister that the man she just saw being dragged across the floor while tied to a grand piano and a rotting donkey carcass is one of the world's greatest artists.

The imbecile just stands calmly, the toothbrush like a pipe in her mouth, until you're finished speaking. Then she says: "But what the fuck is the point?"

The question catches you so unawares that you have no idea what to answer. Bente lingers just long enough to milk it, then turns in triumph and leaves.

Not until you're lying under your duvet with the tingle of Colgate in your mouth—Jesus, Amalie's father told you about an artist who ate his own feces, another who allowed himself to be sprayed with animal blood and sperm, and you, it wouldn't enter your mind to go to bed without having first brushed your teeth!—do you manage to gather your thoughts, and then it wells up, the sentences come thick and fast, each more concise and articulate than the last, the world at your feet, the audience speechless in admiration, Bente and your parents sitting transfixed slap-bang in the middle of the first row.

# "ON THE INADEQUACY OF THE UTILIZATION OF CONCEPTUALIZATION AND THE AUTONOMOUS NATURE OF ART"

Lecture by

## Aksel Morander

 Doors 8:00 PM
Admission 100 Kroner

You're traveling abroad with your parents, on a trip you've known about for several years and which you'd been looking forward to every time you'd thought about it: now, however, it appears to you more like a sojourn in a sauna for three weeks, all while Amalie calls out to you beyond the thick walls. You try to protest, say you don't want to go, say you've decided to stay home instead, that it's a bad time for you just now. Your father looks like the sky has fallen on his head, with his mouth wide open as if faced with some unnatural phenomenon, he stands in front of you and repeats again and again how much the trip has cost him, the tickets, the hotel, and all the rest of the idiotic arrangements. And one week later, as you're walking barefoot on the scorching hot sand, it's with the feeling of being trapped in an enormous cage, infinitely far from the real world, cut off from it, cut off from her, the girl walking around in circles waiting for you on the other side of the globe. It's as though you find yourself in a place where time doesn't pass, while in the real world time tears along, so that as one minute of your incarceration on the Canary Islands has gone by, a day has passed in Amalie's world, and when you have endured an hour in the birdcage, Amalie has endured a year. And you envisage, when the day finally arrives, after five hundred hours, upon your final release, that what's waiting for you back home is an old, unrecognizable, crooked, wrinkled, half-blind woman who's hard of hearing and has long since forgotten the love of her youth.

The others lie on the beach all day, their arms like grilled hotdogs, the hair all over Bente's body turned light yellow, her eyebrows like two bushy accents over that gaping expression of hers when she looks up at you for the umpteenth time and asks why you don't take off your sweater and lie down in the sun as well. It's revolting, the whole beach stinks of suntan oil, naked bodies everywhere, people lying scattered around as if in the wake of a massacre, and the hours are a rout of snails who have just set out on their journey from the far side of the bay. You all eat in the hotel restaurant every evening, at the same table and with the same waiter serving you, a cheeky bastard who flirts openly with both your mother and Bente, without it seeming to bother your father in the slightest. No, on the contrary, by the third or fourth night he's actually encouraging it, as though he's just as honored by the attention as they are. The red lipstick against the sunburnt skin makes them look like hookers, both of them, so maybe it's natural to do it? And no matter how coarse the innuendo from the middle-aged Spaniard, your father just laughs and shrugs and puts his arms out, as if to say: take them, if you like, my women are your women, please, help yourself! Not until the meal is over and you're readying to go, does he dispense with the cheerfulness and become himself again, sullen and reticent, sitting there with his wallet, plucking out coin after coin, in just as much dispute with himself every time about how much it's reasonable to tip.

Even when you've finally got your seatbelt on for the flight home, it's like it's never going to end. The journey lasts and lasts. Dragging on like some final act of evil. The reunion with Amalie appears more distant than ever. Time seems to stack up instead of pass, the minutes being added instead of being taken away.

When the two of you are finally reunited it's as though your own desire finds you inadequate. Nothing is enough. Nothing is capable of satisfying you. You want to put your tongue deeper down her throat, stick your cock even further into her, leave no opening untested, you want to get in everywhere, terrified of missing out on something, convinced that part of her will vanish if you don't ensure you penetrate it as quickly as possible. It's like some terrible hunger has arisen and there's not enough food in the world to satisfy it. Everything is equally tempting. Everything is equally delicious. Your appetite doesn't differentiate. Everything can be eaten, everything can be drunk, everything can be broken, devoured, dissolved and become a part of you. You want to eat and be eaten. You wouldn't waver in a referendum about cannibalism. You want to be eaten and digested by her, your body is a meal, prepared for her, your cannibal goddess, every part of you has her two mouths as objectives, if she so wishes, she can snap every bone in your body, tear your joints right off, fry you over a medium heat, glaze you with your own blood, chew you up into little bits and gnaw every last piece of meat from your bones.

You'd love Amalie to feel the same, that she wanted to eat you too, or be eaten by you, or something even worse, that she came up with something even crazier, you'd love her to say something which made your madness pale in comparison, something which shocked you, which it just wasn't possible to outdo, which drew a definitive line under how much you could possibly need another person. But she doesn't come out with anything like that, nothing besides the usual "I love you" and "I'm so in love with you," which is all well and good but you can't escape the feeling inside telling you they're the kind of things everybody says to one another, no matter how hot or cold their passions may run. You look at her and think: Why don't you let loose on me and scratch me until I bleed? Why don't you scratch yourself until you bleed? Why don't you shout out your love for me? Why don't you cry? Why don't we bawl our eyes out every time we catch sight of one another?

But then she opens up for you, yet again, and your silly thoughts disappear into the urgent pull of the undertow between her legs.

You haven't felt any of this before. It's all been lying buried within you, unused, for want of that which could bring it to life. It's as if you didn't know of what you were composed. Everything you were built of, how the different bits related to one another, which possibilities of sensation lay in every single part, your chest, your stomach, your neck, your coccyx, the eggs in your sack, the seam in the middle, all the way up to the tumescent head, all lay fallow, until she came and placed her hands upon them. She gifted you your body, she initiated you through her touch, roused every body part from death's slumber, one by one, every caress an inception, a blessing. You were a corpse, but you were raised from the grave and brought back to life.

On the nights you sleep at home, alone, you sometimes lie thinking about her for so long that you eventually lose sight of her,
can't remember what she looks like, can't manage to call her face
to mind, like you're thinking her into pieces, thinking about her
so long and hard that in the end you obliterate her completely,
and then, the next day, when you get to school, fearful of being
unable to find her, of discovering she doesn't exist, you'll begin
to search, ask the others if any of them have seen her, and they'll
just shake their heads and start to laugh.

Every Wednesday, during the two-hour break at midday, both of you sit at a table in the very back of the café close to school. Other people from your class stop by too but none of them come over and sit at your table, most of them don't even bother to say hello, as if they understand that the biggest favor they can do the two of you is to ignore you.

"Who's your best friend?" asks Amalie.

She's wearing the yellow coat indoors, the hand-me-down from her mother. It's snowing outside, a cold gust rushes through the locale every time the door opens and closes.

"You!" you answer.

She laughs: "After me then?"

And you think: What kind of question is that to ask? Why should I concern myself with that when I've got you?

She laughs again. "Okay, before we became a couple. Who was your best friend then?"

*A couple*: you'd much rather remark on that, that choice of word, which sounds offensive to your ears, far too weak, far too flimsy and cautious for what the two of you have together. Are you just *a couple*? It sounds so ridiculous, as ridiculous as when you met one of Amalie's aunts in town and she wondered if you were her *beau*.

"In middle school, who was your best friend in middle school?"

"In middle school?" You sigh resignedly. "No one!"

"No one? Didn't you have any friends?"

"Sure . . . I had friends . . . But not proper ones, if that's what you mean . . ."

"Okay, the best one then . . ." She won't give in. "The best one out of all the friends you had."

"No one in particular, really," you say, becoming aware of just how little you want to talk about this. You take a sip of tea to give yourself time to think. "I was just happy when it was finished and I didn't have to have anything else to do with them."

She raises her eyebrows.

"Was it that bad?"

You shrug.

"They were a bunch of bastards, the whole lot of them."

"Jesus! They can't all have been that bad? I mean, there must have been a few who . . ."

"No!" you say, more sternly than you'd intended: "There wasn't."

Then, in a milder tone: "There wasn't."

She looks utterly bewildered. You wish the two of you could talk about something else, something that would draw her back toward you, not drive her away. You lay your hand on the table. She waits a moment then takes it.

"But now I've got you," you say, squeezing her hand. She smiles, but you can see her mind is at full tilt behind her eyes. A little window is glowing in each of her pupils, in the center of the windows there's a tiny black curl with the café logo.

"In elementary school, then?" She asks, and for the first time you're aware of something resembling annoyance: she won't drop it.

"In elementary school . . ." you say, and mostly in the hope of putting an end to the interrogation, "I had a friend. A best friend."

"Who?"

"Oskar."

"Who's Oskar?"

"Social Science. Tall thin guy, dark curly hair."

"Oskar Wang?"

You nod.

"The two of you were best friends?"

"Yeah."

"But you never talk to one another!"

"No, not now."

"Why not?"

You grimace.

"You both *go* to the same school! You *see* one another every day!"

"I know."

"You were best friends and now you don't even acknowledge one another . . . ?"

"People change," you say.

"I guess . . ." she says.

Actually you want to ask her what she thinks of it but you let it go and instead say: "Fried egg on a plate without the plate."

She laughs, but the seriousness is still there, she's still thinking about the same thing, there doesn't appear to be anything that will distract her from it.

"What about you, then?" you ask, to be on the safe side. "Who's *your* best friend?"

As soon as you ask she turns even more serious, frowns and appears to give the matter serious consideration. It takes ages. In the end you begin to feel slightly uneasy, she just sits there, the same expression on her face, thinking and thinking.

Then, finally, she looks up.

"You!" she says, and then she can't contain herself any longer, her features explode in laughter, she pokes you in the stomach and you feel stupid for having been fooled.

# Everybody Has Loved
# Life at One Time

It's the first day of middle school, the room is new, the teacher is new, but the class is the same, even the seating arrangement is the same, everyone at the same desks, as though it hadn't occurred to anyone to switch, to change anything at all. And you know: life is stale, development has stopped up, all that awaits you and the twenty-six others is an endless repetition of the same, always the same. The sun shines harshly through the windows leaving nothing in peace, and there's something about the way Oskar looks at you that lets you know how things are going to be, today and all the days to come. Already in the first period, as you're taking turns introducing yourselves, he gets the better of you. Gretha is sitting behind you and has just finished telling the new teacher about herself when you hear Oskar's voice, just a sigh, almost inaudible, and not intended for anyone other than you. And he knows well that you'll hear it, that you won't be able to help registering that derisive, slightly resigned tone. You don't have sense enough to try and ignore him and turn to meet his gaze. And when you look back at the teacher you know that Oskar is watching your every move, that he'll take note of everything you do and everything you say, every little detail. And you know that no matter what passes your lips you'll get in a muddle, that no matter how you begin it'll come out wrong. And then you say it, your name, so low that the teacher has to ask you to repeat it. And at the same moment you submit to what you know will come, just as though your name alone is enough to turn up the heat in your head. You bring your hand to your face, pretend to rest your chin on your fingers, try to conceal it, even though you know the battle is lost, that everything you say from now on will only make the red color deeper and stronger, that every word you utter will increase the heat and that there's nothing in this world to help hide it, no hands, no clothes, no hats, no hair, no clever diversions, not if a hole had opened up beneath you, not if a giant hand had come in the window and picked you up. The bright red color is a fact. Your scarlet face is noted and logged. You sit there in the middle of the clatter and rattle of a power plant of pure red, luminous and radiant as a panic-stricken angel, as a fiery red beet, for the whole world to see.

One reading = five minutes. One row = six desks. Six desks = thirty minutes. If Oftedal begins at your row at the front you'll have to read, if he begins from the back, then the chances are you'll be spared. And if one happy period should elapse without you having to read aloud or say anything, if you manage to avoid the attention of the teacher and the rest of the class for forty-five glorious minutes, then Oskar is there, like some considerate bastard, to ensure the redness is shown to its best advantage all the same. He doesn't need to do anything other than let his presence be known, remind you he's there keeping an eye on you. At other times he uses sign language to signal the word for blushing, like the biology teacher taught you all. Or at a moment where Oftedal is not on his guard he makes a wisecrack at your expense. And it works every time. You can't look in Oskar's direction without your blood beginning to surge. He can do what he wants with you, he need only look at you and it spreads all the way up to your hairline, it couldn't be any worse if he was sitting holding a fucking remote control beneath his desk.

You can envisage it, your circulation transporting the hateful blood around your body, back and forth along interminable sections, clattering freight trains thundering through the red glow of signal lights, up and down the shiny rails linking the parts of your body to the red-hot totality you're made up of, the bright, burning entirety there's no getting away from, the only person you wish had never been born, the only person you wish it was not possible to be.

To be an astronaut, you think, to be packed within an enormous padded, pressurized outfit that conceals everything, floating weightlessly somewhere in outer space, fired out like a missile, en route to the unknown, further and further from Earth, leaving behind everything that pulls you down, free from all the misery, leaving it behind like a lump of shit on a green and blue marble, a little stone, a particle of sand, just a speck of dust, finally smaller than a speck, finally nothing.

The schoolyard at night, now free of life, free of the clamor, of the fighting, the ganging-up and the name-calling, seems desolate and abandoned, redolent of an army barracks everyone has fled in haste. What if it was always like this, you think. Empty. Quit. Vacated. What if every city could be emptied of its inhabitants. What if the whole world could be evacuated.

On a gravel pitch, down from a small incline on the edge of the school property, a football match is in full swing. The sound of shouting, swearing and jubilant yells carry up to your hiding place behind the high wire fence as if from far away: every time someone strikes the ball cleanly the sound only reaches you a second or so after. The longer you observe them the more people from class you recognize, in the end there's only two or three you can't identify. A small group of girls are standing by one goalpost watching. Every time there's a coming together, or the beginnings of a quarrel, Oskar is the one who intervenes and sorts it out. And when one of the others is alone on the keeper and gets brought down from behind, everybody lines up on the edge of the penalty area waiting for Oskar, as though it couldn't occur to them that anyone other than him would take the kick.

It grows darker, the air gets chillier, the game continues with unabated intensity, but it's as though the sounds from the riotous struggle down on the gravel diminish more and more, even though there are only so many meters separating you from your classmates. And while you sit like that spying on them, you remember the feeling you always had when you were with Oskar, that feeling of exuberance that spread in your blood, which at that time coursed calmly through your body without ever being anywhere near your face, just as though something flowed from you and combined with a corresponding something which flowed from Oskar, something you had always had within you, but had to keep to yourself, hold back, subdue, keep under wraps, prevent from spilling out from you, because it was dangerous, because you knew you'd end up lying there bleeding to death if you let it happen. But suddenly the connection was there, the one you hadn't been aware you needed, the one Oskar brought with him, that arose the moment Oskar walked with you on the first day of school, as if from then on the two of you had mingled blood every hour, every minute you were together, as if the same blood had been running through you both in all the years before you met, trapped in each closed circuit, and that now, finally the two of you made it to that place where you could open yourselves and let it flow, without being afraid of anything, without fear of death, without fear of the world, without the slightest trace of apprehension of anything at all.

It's the same every time: after having set you all some idiotic task
at the workbenches, Paulsen disappears for the rest of the class,
and from the moment that old sot with the potato nose goes out
the door, lawlessness reigns. Everybody soon drops what they
were doing, not because they've got anything better to do but
because they can't help it. Oskar is irrepressible. He comes out
with one story after the next, as though he's rehearsed beforehand. Systematically, as if following a plan, he goes through
everything you and he had together and ridicules it. You knew
it: you should never have let yourself in for it. It was too good to
be true, in reality you were aware of that, something was trying
to tell you that from the start, but you were too eager, you didn't
listen, didn't want to listen, allowed the din of all that was good
to drown it out. Everything is doomed, so was this, the difference
was Oskar understood it before you. He got out in time. And
now he's reaping the fruits of his foresight. He mimics you, how
you fired back with the radium gun when you were John Carter.
He does an impression of your Phantom voice. He shows them
how you taped a toothpick across your lip to look like Jonah
Hex. You try to laugh along with them, try to make it look like
you're not bothered, even when you hear completely twisted
versions of things you yourself are supposed to have said, you
try to act like you find it amusing to listen to, but to no avail, it
flows to your head and reveals you.

Blood. Your fucking blood. Your mutinous blood. The blood that's your curse, because it's visible, because it seeps through that all-too-thin wrapping of yours, that all-revealing film of facial skin, which makes you transparent, which means everything that normal people exercising a little willpower are able to conceal, to keep in check, is written all across your face in flaming letters instead, a plain text in bright red which turns you inside out, leaving no one without in any doubt as to how things are with you within.

You take a box cutter from your father's tool shelf in the garage, bring it with you into the woods, snap off the endmost section of the blade and adjust its sharp replacement so it sticks out just a couple of millimeters. Then you press it against your forearm, up by the elbow, grit your teeth and bring the yellow handle in a straight line almost to your wrist bone. At first it burns, as though barbed wire is being drawn through your arm. Then all you feel is a faint chill. Your skin opens, the blood appearing after a moment, pumping calmly out into a neat stream that follows the path of the knife. It feels like a relief. *My arm is a pipe that can be drained of blood. My arm is an object fixed to a body. My arm sticks out like an implement that can be employed in some way. My arm is bleeding, good, it's about time.* You turn your arm over, stick the tip in below your wrist bone and make a new thin track in the opposite direction. You envisage that if you bleed out a sufficient amount, there won't be enough left to send to your head. You draw yet another two channels, and it's strange, because it's as though the cuts aren't visible, like the dark blood isn't coming from any particular place, as though it's just flowing across your arm, without having anything to do with it.

Then you don't remember anything except waking up on the ground with your ear pressed against a tree root. It's cold, you're freezing, your body feels battered. You glance at your arm, which looks like it's covered in black fur. You've no feeling in it, as though it's lying there in the foliage on its own. You lift it. Grass and leaves accompany it, stuck fast to the congealed blood. You feel like you're about to pass out again. You sink back, lie down and stare up at the huge sky, vaulting above with an inaudible roar, inaudible for you and for everyone else, inaudible in the same way that nobody can hear you lying there by yourself on that rotting forest floor. No one knows you're there, no one knows what you've done, no one knows what you're thinking, no one will ever know anything about you, your thoughts, your desires, no one will ever have any knowledge of the hopelessness and sorrow your life consists of. You are hopeless but no one knows that. You cry out in despair, but no one hears it, nor do you.

As a further insult, you're unable to interpret it in any other way, Oskar becomes best friends with Stein-Ove. They start hanging around with each other at breaks, inseparable, a new couple, middle school's Oskar and Stein-Ove, like a grotesque parody of elementary school's Oskar and Aksel. And one Monday morning, as you're sitting in the locker room getting changed for PE, you hear them laughing and joking about the weekend, how many fizzy drinks they've consumed and how many sweets they've managed to stuff themselves with, as though the purpose of the conversation is for you to overhear it. But then they lower their voices, Oskar leans forward and says something to Stein-Ove, you can't catch what, and they look over at you, both of them, and grin.

The last quarter of an hour of PE is, as usual, given over to floorball. You and Stein-Ove are constantly bumping into one another, as though he's seeking you out on purpose and trying to engineer a collision. But at one stage you manage to grab the ball from him and by an unbelievable stroke of luck, the pass you make right after turns out to be an assist.

He comes over to you in the showers afterwards, stands in front of you, stark naked, hands at his side, his eyes fixed on your bandaged arm. Then he says: "What the fuck is with you?" Behind him, over by the benches, Oskar stands drying off, following the scene.

"Are you a homo or something?" says Stein-Ove.

You don't answer.

He makes to reach for your crotch. You pull away, banging into the soap holder and knocking the shampoo down. Stein-Ove laughs. Then he turns serious again.

"I've never seen you piss at the urinal," he says. "Is that because you're afraid?"

You turn off the water and try to get past. Stein-Ove blocks your way.

"Huh? Afraid you'll get a hard-on?"

He presses his fingertips into your shoulder and gives you a shove.

"Is that why?"

Then he takes hold of his own dick and simulates beating off, even though it's limp.

"Do you want to blow me? Do you?"

He gives you another shove on the shoulder and continues with the jerking off.

"I asked you a question. Do you want to blow me?"

Several of the other boys have gathered around the two of you. You stand quite still, not lifting a finger, while Stein-Ove repeats the question. Suddenly he throws both his arms around you and begins riding your leg like a dog. You can feel his limp genitals slapping against your thigh. More boys come to look, laughter resounds.

"Ooh, I'm gonna come!" Stein-Ove cries out in a falsetto voice. "Ooh, Aksel! So good! I'm coming!"

Your only friend, the box cutter, is with you everywhere. Should things get too bad, you think. It gives you a warm feeling, thinking about the friendship of the only one who'll be there to take care of you. A few days go by between each time you dare to use it, there's something repugnant about sticking the knife in the old cuts, they look like puckered mouths full of smashed teeth. At the same time there's something enjoyable about that sickening sensation, making you feel pale, faded, anemic, drained of energy and consequently, you think, drained of blood. You make a few short incisions between the longer ones, making it look like a ladder and think surely it must be possible to get right to the bottom by way of it.

Then, all at once, on the way home from school, he appears beside you, as if nothing has happened, as though there's no ill feeling between you, like you're back where you left off. You listen attentively, steal glances at him and try to discern the irony no doubt lying behind. But no, not the slightest trace of the asshole is to be found in anything he says as you pass the beer barrel by the steps down to the restaurant by the waterfall and the packet of butter on the roof of the margarine factory, the only magical objects in this sad town of timber houses.

He seems quite sincere. You have no choice other than to take him seriously. Incredible but true. Suddenly everything's as it was. Suddenly nothing is in the way. You picture it, how the city's coat of arms on the Mesna bridge is nearly hidden from view by all the vegetation growing along the riverbanks, coiling like bunches of barbed wire around the wrought-iron decorations along the railing, how the sign with the arrow for the Mesna Factory is only legible due to being embossed, how the facade of the Kronen Hotel is stippled by plants growing wild and the statue of Wiese is protruding from the ground like a chocolate figure someone's taken a bite of. You're both back on the Planet of the Apes. Finally you've returned. Everything is as before. Everything is as it was. The people passing you on the pavement are like shadows. It's as though nothing around you really exists. The whole town is like that, like a badly painted backdrop hung up around your and Oskar's world. When the two of you overhear somebody say something, it sounds like a dialogue from a play they've put on, one about life in a tragic little town, a tiny speck on the map, full of miserable, hapless individuals doomed long ago.

At night you lie in bed, elated at the disappearance of your tormentor and the return of your best friend, so worked up and wide awake that it's as though you have the night behind you and not in front, you have the vague notion of using up time to sleep as totally meaningless, dreams as boring routine, all you want is for the night to pass and the light to return, that it will begin to rise like transparent water outside your window, that it will finally be daytime again and Oskar will be standing waiting for you at the gate like he used to, ready for the decisive battle against three thousand Ptothians who've just broken through the lines of Jedwar, Supreme Commander of the Orovar army.

The next day you're on a school trip to a wilderness wildlife museum a couple of hours away, and as you all sit crammed together around an oval table in the museum café, with chalk-white walls surrounding you, white light from the ceiling above, everything bright and perceptible, you notice Oskar, who's sitting across from you and is just finished eating, crumpling the sandwich paper into a ball while glancing around, a restless look in his eyes. You can see it, how pent-up he is, restless, how he needs to torment again, how too much time has passed and it's like oxygen to him. You tense up, prepare yourself for the ball of paper in the face at any moment. Instead Oskar contents himself with holding your gaze, knowing he doesn't need to do any more. And you feel it: the blood-letting hasn't helped, your body is just as full of that shitty fluid as it's always been, as a new charge begins to bubble up around your neck, ready to be sent up to your face. To occupy your hands you begin to scratch your forearm. And with a resigned expression, like he's starting to tire of it but still feels duty call, Oskar smiles and says in a loud voice so everyone can hear: "Itching to get back to it, Aksel?"

You look around at the night of your youth. You can hear a rumbling sound, like the approach of a thousand tank treads. The ground shakes. And what is that gigantic monument that suddenly looms above? A colossus, an immense black tower, with a red light at the top, blocks your path, so high there's no way over, so wide there's no way around. You're the colossus, you yourself stand there blocking the road, so that you can never move forward in life, not as who you are, not as who you'd like to be, not as someone you could imagine being. There's no way through. Everything is closed off. The tower stands tall and somber above you, your house, and your neighborhood, above the schoolyard, the town, and the world, casting its shadow over everything and covering it in darkness.

You look around at the night of your youth. Nothing good is left. Lillehammer has been transformed into a sewer, the streets are filled with shit, piss, and crumpled newspapers people have wiped their backsides with; it's swarming with green blowflies and fat tapeworms; it reeks, everything's filthy, nothing's good. You can picture it. And you hate it. You hate all people. You hate everything living, everything that helps keep things alive. You hate your heart for continuing to beat, you hate your lungs for drawing in that contaminated air no matter what, your eyes which never stop looking, your hands which are never at rest, your fingers which are unable to cease, which flex and stretch a thousand times a day, which are unstoppable, which are busy touching and scratching things all the time.

You want to tell someone, you want to break down in someone's arms and tell them everything. But who? Oftedal? Your parents? And what would you say? What is there to tell? That Oskar is looking at you during class? That he clears his throat? That he sighs loudly? That he makes the sign for blush in sign language? That he smacks his lips and makes clicking sounds with his tongue? That he says your name all the time? That he mumbles it, whispers it and mouths it? If only you were being beaten, you think. If only you had bruises to take home, some injuries to point to, a broken arm, a missing tooth. If only Oskar went for you one day in front of everyone, attacked you and gave you such a going over that you couldn't get to your feet afterwards. You want to be knocked to the ground and beaten senseless: being peppered with punches and kicks, you imagine, would be a good place to be. If only the battering was brutal enough it would be your salvation. You fantasize about permanent injury and the resultant sympathy. The hospital, what a lovely place! Lying in an ocean of tubes, connected up to all types of machines, fed by spoon and straw, anxious faces around the bed every time you come around from dozing. You fantasize about sustaining such serious injuries that they need to wrap bandages all around your head. You dream about being like The Invisible Man, with sunglasses, a hat and a little hole for your mouth. You'd be fearless then, in the company of other people, if the whole of your face and body were bandaged. How happy and carefree you'd be, if you were able to walk around like a living mummy. How easily you'd cope with Oskar, how effortlessly you'd conduct yourself in the classroom, how naturally you'd act and how exuberant you'd be in every social situation.

On the way to school, out for a drive in the car with your parents, alone in your room with a book you're trying to concentrate on, in bed at night before you sleep, no matter where you are you picture how it ought to be, how things would be if justice were to be found. Oskar bound hand and foot in the drum of a giant meat grinder, or fleeing in desperation down ever-narrowing corridors with razor blades fixed to the walls. Oskar being stretched on a rack, his knees crackling, whimpering for mercy. Salt water being injected into his veins. Sewage being emptied down his throat. His ribs being cracked one by one with a hammer and chisel. His balls being cut up. Testicles crushed in a vice. Ears sawn off with a hacksaw. His nails prized up like little lids and yanked out. His eyeballs scooped out with a spoon. Tongue cut off with a scissors, his skull bored with a drill. Just like in *Weird Tales* magazine, where evil is always punished and where the fate villains meet is always just as bad or worse than the wickedness they themselves are responsible for.

At night, if he's indoors, you bring Festus with you to your room and try to get him to lie by your head, or under the duvet with you, but the idiot of a cat just twists loose, as though in disgust, and migrates to the end of the bed where he treads a hollow in the duvet and settles down in the natural depression between your legs. If you're sitting on the sofa in the living room, he sometimes comes and lies down beside you. But if you reach out to try and stroke him he gets up and immediately jumps down. It drives you mad, his weird fear of touch, it's like he never allows you the physical contact you crave, just about, always just about. Sometimes, if you're quick, you can just barely manage to give his head a rub before he runs off, nauseous with delight you feel that tiny skull between your fingers for a second or two. You can't understand why he doesn't want to be caressed, nor why, when he doesn't, he still comes and lies down near you. But he's quite consistent. He seeks company but rejects intimacy. He wants to be with you but not close to you.

You're sitting upside down in the sofa with your legs over the back of it: there's something good about looking at everything turned on its head. You fantasize about walking around in the freedom of the large white room while looking up at the crammed ceiling, thinking how nice it would be if it had looked like that, how new and unfamiliar it would be, all of it, nothing left of the way it was. You sit like that, entranced, until your temples feel like they're going to burst, then you straighten up from your moment of bliss, dizzy, and remain sitting in the sofa for a while, completely still, while your blood, which you have way too much of, sinks back and reality, which is unbearable, falls into place around you.

Festus suddenly appears there, standing in the center of the orange part of the carpet on the living room floor, the one filled with flames or snakes when you were small, and he's looking at you with that damned Mona Lisa smile of his, his tail straight up like an exclamation mark. You feel like doing something, but don't know what. The knife is pressing against your thigh. You take it from your pocket, open your zip, pull out your dick and make a cut right at the base, then sit there with it in your hand while you picture the blood gush and feel how the pressure diminishes, how your body would become lighter and freer for every liter that flowed from you.

And you picture the colossus changed into a steamroller, that instead of standing below it looking up, you're sitting in it looking down, a load of levers and a huge steering wheel in front of you, and that the noise from the engine is deafening, and that everything you head for is squeezed flat beneath you. You drive through woodland and over large residential areas. A broad belt of flattened houses lies in your wake, trimmed with squashed human mince. Eventually you reach the school, and without stopping crash through the wall and head across the schoolyard, where the playground equipment snaps like toothpick models. You allow yourself a breather outside building C, sitting for a while in the vibrating driver's cab, looking at the windows far below where you can just about make out a couple of your classmates, then you put it in gear, slip the clutch and put your foot down, the whole steamroller lurches forward, and the three-story building folds like cardboard while blood spurts out from every side. The monster machine crawls up the incline at the back of the school, dragging a large section of the wire fence with it on its way. You swing around in the direction of the town center, you picture Main Street packed with busy people and feel a tingling in your chest at the thought of what lies ahead of you, while the enormous metal cylinder spins and spins beneath you the whole time, mangling everything in its way.

Your father comes into your room one evening. You're sitting under your Donald Duck lamp, reading, completely engrossed (Smith's group have just landed in the deep mountain snow, the Eagles' Nest only a day's march away), torn from your own world and welcomed like a hero to another (war: what a good place to be!) and you can tell by the look of him that he's on a mission of his own, dispatched by your mother in all likelihood, and afterwards you think about how he'd probably much rather have been parachuted out over the German-occupied Alps than have had to have gone into his son's room that night.

He sits down awkwardly on the side of the bed. "Listen, Aksel," he says, clearing his throat. Then clears it again, slaps his huge hand on his knee and begins massaging his thigh.

He sits like that for a moment.

Then he says: "I don't know. If you've covered that stuff in school. About reproduction?"

"Yeah, we have," you hurry to reply: "We had it just a while ago." And then it comes, the blushing which for a moment there you felt you could control: the temperature in the room increases by a few degrees, you feel you could have heated up a whole house.

"Okay!" your dad says, with obvious relief, clapping you on the shoulder and getting to his feet. It's like a different man is standing there, you can't remember having seen him so happy. *Mission accomplished.* And yet he just remains standing there. Is it because your mother is in the living room waiting? Is that why he feels obliged to stay a little longer, to avoid at all costs giving the impression that he's taken his responsibilities too lightly. No, he really isn't showing any sign of wanting to go. He stands with his hands by his sides, surveying the entire room, studying everything, the posters on the walls, the bookshelves, the furniture, as if he were a prospective buyer.

You sit with the book open in your lap, picking at your sleeve, enjoying the prickling of the little scabs coming loose underneath, uncertain as to whether you can continue reading or if that'll be taken as an insult.

Then he turns to you.

"Is there anything else you were wondering about?"

You shrug.

"Nothing?"

Then you say: "Do people change?"

"What?" he says.

"Does it happen that people change? Or are you the same your whole life through?"

Your father grins.

"Is that from the book you're reading or something?"

Then he looks at his watch. "Well, I guess I better . . ."

He walks over and opens the door, and is already halfway out when he sticks his head back in.

"Good luck, then," he says.

That night you lie there thinking about all the things you should have said, all the things you could have asked him to do, to have spoken to the headmaster and tried to get Oskar expelled, or suspended, or persuaded him to organize a transfer to another class, for either Oskar or you, it doesn't matter, as long as you're separated, as long as it meant you'd avoid having anything else to do with one another, as long as something happened which brought about a change, which put an end to the relationship between you. Or if it was possible to switch schools? If they could arrange it so you went to a different school for the remainder of middle school, in another town if necessary, you'd be fine with that, no problem at all, there's sure to be a bus, other people have to commute after all, have to travel a total of a couple of hours back and forth every single day. You wouldn't have anything against getting up at dawn or having to travel a good way off, on the contrary it'd be an absolute pleasure, something you did with the greatest joy, no matter how far it might be, every early morning bus ride would be a victory march considering everything you were spared. And you think: This is all because we sit next to one another. Everything is like this because our desks are beside one another in that torture chamber that's called a classroom. If I'd been sitting in the back of the row by the windows and he'd been at the top of the row by the wall, everything would have been different, then none of this would have needed to happen, then the situation would have been quite different, then I might never have known that things could be like this. And eventually you've given this entire other world, the one which will grant you your life back, so much long and hard thought, that the one around you has ceased to exist, nothing of it remains, your room is an empty shell, a sketch someone has drawn in order for it to look like there's something there, just like the rest of the house, the rest of the town, the school, the church, the town hall and all the shops, the only real thing is Festus, who has coiled up in the peaceful hollow at the end of the duvet, lying there with all his weight, making it feel like you have a block of cement around your feet, ready to be taken on a boat ride by the Mob.

To be a cat, you think, your whole face covered in fur, unperturbed by everything around you, aloof and arrogant, disposed toward nothing other than perpetual repetition of the same things, sleep and wake, sleep and wake, without regard for anyone or anything. And you think: Why am I Aksel and not Festus? What reason is there for it to actually turn out that way? Why isn't it the other way around? And suddenly, at the very moment the thought occurs something miraculous happens: You become Festus and Festus becomes you! You switch places right there and then. All of a sudden he's lying beneath the duvet, stretched out in human form, while you're lying on top of him, curled around your own furry body, down in the hollow between his feet.

Incredible! Your dream has come to pass! The transformation has taken place! But since neither of you can recollect what you were before, and since your new selves have no memories or feelings other than those already present, the cat in your case and the human in Festus's, then neither of you notice any difference, and everything carries on as before, even after such a fantastic event.

"Seriously. What's with him?" Bente asks. The two of you are at the table waiting for dinner, and without thinking about it you've once again begun to pick at the sleeve of your sweater. You feel the insects crawling within your arm, nibbling at your bones like ants under the bark of a tree, and the attention of your sister, unaccustomed as you are to it, makes the whole room light up, leaving no nook or cranny left to hide in, all the light, every ray is concentrated on you, everything points toward you in the illuminated center. "Jesus," you hear her groan, from far off, "Can't you just have a word with him or something?" She talks about you as if you're not there anymore. And she's right, you think, you are lost to them, cast out, with all hope gone and you can no longer expect anything from that quarter.

You're home alone, but you're too restless to get anything done, can't really get into anything the way you used to, just wander about, glancing out the window toward the driveway, listening for the crunch of car wheels on the gravel. In the absence of being able to think up anything else to do, you take up a few stones and try to hit the birdhouse in the neighbors' tree. Then you go into the garage, turn on the light and see the strict composition of your father's world fall into place, piece by piece, in the clicking and blinking of the fluorescent tubes. In one corner, next to where some gardening tools neatly hang, there's a bunch of old weapons: a bow and arrow, a spear, a sword, a shield you made in woodworking class, sticks and lengths of wood with bent nails as triggers and a weapon of greater workmanship that your father made, and which had conferred a degree of status on you among your pals in the last place you had lived. There's a layer of dust, as well as fine woodchip from the lathe covering everything; they look like the appropriated spoils from a war fought centuries ago.

You wander around the garden. By the flowerbed beside the outdoor grill, Festus is lying on the ground with something dark squeezed between his paws. He peeps up at you, with obvious pride, picking a little at the mauled animal, a ripple of glee passing through him each time, and after a while he stares at the lifeless little body in surprise, taken aback that the moment of glee has passed. Eventually he realizes that the struggle is over, sinks his teeth into the neck of his prey and bites off the head.

You crouch down next to Festus, who's still busy chewing. You reach out and pick up a stone from the ones bordering the flowerbed. It's heavy, you let it rest on your thigh. You lift your other hand, placing it gently over Festus's neck. He doesn't take any notice. His jaws are working slowly and steadily. He swallows, and sniffs a little, then takes the rest of the mouse in his mouth. You tighten your grip around his neck, feel him give a start as though from an electric shock. He tugs and twitches but you hold tight. Then you raise the stone above his head, close your eyes and bring it down. You hear the most awful wail. You feel a burning scratch across the knuckles. You have to use all your strength to hold him tight. You feel tears begin to build up. Then you lift the stone and bring it down once more. You repeat the motion, up and down with the stone, which is so large you can barely get your hand around it.

The wail turns to wheezing, then a few dry hacks. The twitching subsides. It feels like you're holding a bag that's been emptied of its contents. You wait until there's nothing left in it. Then you open your eyes. Festus's head is completely flat. The mouse's tail is sticking out of his jaw, which has come a bit away from the rest of his head. You get up and toss the bloody stone over the fence. You dry your tears with an unstained patch of the sleeve of your sweater. It's strange to look at, the body, which was alive just a little while ago, showing no sign of life, like the cat has been dead for several days. You take hold and lift him up. He feels heavier now than you remember, like the weight of some dead mechanism, of a large complicated piece of equipment that's broken down.

You carry him over to the rubbish bins, open the lid and shove him far down among the smooth bags. Then you walk back over to the grill. A dark patch in the grass is all that shows. You bend down. It takes a little while before you notice that there's something there, in the brown, sticky mess, a small eye peering up at you. You feel nausea spread like a chill through your chest, your larynx swelling, but nothing comes up, just remains in your throat like a cold crowbar, just like there's nothing coming from the eye, no gaze, no life, just the bland reflection of the light hitting it, as though from any object at all that someone had been unlucky enough to lose. You look at one another. And you realize that there's nothing in anything, not in you, not in anything around you, nor in the people around you either, everything is empty, everything is lackluster and dead, everything's a waste.

As if comfort were to be found in the hard facts, your father attempts to elucidate the headstrong nature of cats, while your mother seems chiefly offended by Festus just running off without letting her know beforehand. Bente doesn't say anything, but going by the looks she sends you, you could almost believe she knew something, or suspected something. On the other hand it may be that she's just got used to always thinking the worst about you?

Your hope is that Oskar will grow tired of it. That it'll bore him in the long run, picking on the same person day after day, and that sooner or later, for the sake of a challenge, he'll find someone else to take it out on. And in eighth grade, around Christmas, it's like they've already become a little duller, a little weaker, those jibes of his, as if there's something uninspiring or joyless about them, as though they've ceased to amuse him, that he's only doing it from force of habit. It's like he's actually lost interest in getting at you but can't help doing it, he does it without thinking, in the same way he eats a packed lunch or goes to the toilet. Oskar's lack of spirit becomes your strength, the monotonous repetition has over time made you gradually more resistant. Just as it's become a habit for the one doing it, it's become a habit for the one it's directed at. Just six months more! you think. Max! And in the false security of this hope, you begin, almost stealthily, proceeding as though it's only a question of time until it's over.

At Easter you get together with Unn, a girl from the year under, who's holidaying with her family in the same place as you: far from home, and without thought to the consequences, you let yourself fall in love. The last night in the mountains she cries, because her family have to leave, because the two of you are to part. You sit by the fire in the hotel reception, holding each other by the hand, the crackling heat casting a safe, golden glow.

On the night you arrive home, you lock the door of the basement toilet, remove your sweater and begin peeling off the plasters, carefully. Only when you're in the shower, after a good quantity of pink water has met in a bloody star at the drain, does your arm begin to resemble a part of your body again, gray skin traversed by long irritated ridges with steps between, and again you think about that ladder that appears, which you thought led downwards, that maybe it can be turned around, that maybe it's possible to use it to climb upwards as well?

He doesn't pay any attention to you in the whole of the first class after Easter holidays, his attention is elsewhere, Stein-Ove and he are up to something. You notice him looking at you a couple of times, but you don't care, don't turn around, just carry on with your own thing. You feel unfazed, feel strong, feel that you can manage, feel like your blood has calmed, is equally distributed between all the parts of your body, and isn't collecting at your neck like in a corked bottle. I'm badass, you think as the bell goes for the end of the first class. I'm going to do this. During the break you see Unn on the other side of the school yard, but you don't have the nerve to go over to her. She catches sight of you, you can see that, but she doesn't acknowledge you, nor smile, nor wave. You've no idea how to take it, if it's an understandable precaution or if there's another more terrible intention behind it.

When you come back in for the second class, Oskar's eyes follow you from the moment you appear in the doorway until you sit down at your desk. You see it right away, it's good old Oskar sitting there. Tormentor. Derider. Piss-taker. Ready to get down to it again. And in the end you can't help but turn around. Oskar is like an inflated balloon, his eyes look like they're going to pop out of his head, and he has difficulty keeping a straight face when he asks: "Nice holiday?"

A couple of girls from your class come over and ask: "Aren't you together with Unn, then?" "Unn?" you reply, trying to sound surprised. "The ugly one, you mean?"

You see Oskar in the background, following the scene from a distance, having probably sent the girls over and told them what to say. You haven't spoken to Unn since the holiday. And one day you hear how she's told her friends that you tried to rape her at Easter, that she'd only just managed to get away.

The guy everyone calls Zombie is the one who tells you this. Why him exactly? You've never had any dealings with one another, have never exchanged a word, in fact you've hardly even considered him someone in the class, not before he comes over, stands beside you and starts talking. A revolting smell hits you. You've smelt it before, but only faintly. It's the reason he's left alone and nobody in the class bothers him. Everybody talked about it on the first day, how he stank, but then they were done with him and left him in peace.

The first thing Zombie says is the thing about Unn, that's the reason he's come over. But you don't perceive any malice behind it. It seems like he's telling you because he feels it's unreasonable that you're unaware of what's being said, of how people are talking about you, of the rumors doing the rounds. Then he tells you that he lives with his aunty and uncle, and that he's just been given the whole basement to have all to himself, and that they let him do whatever he wants, as long as he keeps it down. He was wondering if you'd like to come over some time and see his place. And then he grins, as if he now considers you equals, the two of you, that after that story about Unn you're held in just as low regard as him, that now you're both outcasts then the two of you may as well join forces and have done with it: Us against the rest, eh? is what he's saying to you, with his inane, foul-smelling smirk. You turn to look at him. He has a face full of spots, even under his greasy fringe you can discern a forest of tiny plums. His eyes are blank, his face expressionless, like that of a snowman melting in spring.

The smell at his place is the same as the one you get when he brushes by you at school. Zombie puts on a Uriah Heep tape. The picture on the cover is creepy: a man with his mouth wide open and his face covered in spiderwebs, and you think about how you'll end up looking like that if you breathe in his stench too long.

"Batten down the hatches!" he suddenly calls out, holds his nose, bends his knees and lets rip. He subsequently sniffs it in with feigned relish. You grin, even though you don't feel like it. You don't really want to. But you do it all the same, so as not to disappoint him. You're not up for any of this, but now you're here and you have to stay, you have to do as the situation demands. It's a mistake, you know that, it's all wrong from the get-go, but you're already on your way.

He motions for you to come over to a wardrobe in the bedroom, waiting until you're right beside it before opening the door. A vast collection of magazines spills out into a tempting fan at your feet, pale bodies lying on top of and beneath one another, like in a mass grave. Zombie rummages through the pile, picks one out and hands it to you. You take a quick look through it. "Or what about this one?" he smirks, giving you another. You both know what you feel like doing yet the two of you take a long time getting around to it.

You don't quite remember how it came about. But you can conjure up the image, the two of you sitting on the sofa with your trousers around your ankles and a magazine each. The embarrassment is instantaneous, as Zombie passes you the kitchen roll you dare not look at him, just fix yourself up hurriedly and make up your mind to head off and act like you don't know him the next time he invites you back home. But before another hour has passed, the pants are off again, as though all both of you have been doing in the meantime is waiting around gathering the strength for another bout.

The two of you are in front of the mirror, you're wearing a pair of beige high-heeled boots and an ankle-length black dress with red and silver embroidery, Zombie has red long johns on with blue swimming trunks over, a yellow hoody, blue ski gloves, and an old slalom helmet. The volume is so loud the window frames are rattling. Zombie is posing with a shield and a scimitar he made in woodwork, leaning toward his reflection, knees bent, as if ready to attack, while you stand in the background swaying from side to side. Both of you are miming.

*I need someone to show me*
*The things in life that I can't find*
*I can't see the things that make true happiness*
*I must be blind*

*Make a joke and I will sigh*
*And you will laugh and I will cry*
*Happiness I cannot feel*
*And love to me is so unreal*

*And so as you hear these words*
*Telling you now of my state*
*I tell you to enjoy life*
*I wish I could but it's too late*

Zombie steals from his aunty and uncle and always has money handy, every sleepover starts with a shopping trip where you load up on fizzy drinks, crisps, and sweets, as much as you can carry and stuff your faces the whole night, until your bellies are sticking out and the flesh is as taut as a drum. Zombie plays you a tape that he's recorded his own farts on, the two of you lie on the floor shrieking with laughter at every high-pitched meow, every deep, drawn-out machine gun salvo, some of which seem like they'll never end. When you go to bed, Zombie suggests a farting competition, based on who can make one last the longest. You come close to beating him. And when you stick your head under the duvet later and sniff, it's his smell you get.

Both of you are wanking, you on the sofa, Zombie in the arm-chair across, when, in a groggy voice, he asks if he can try some-thing out. You say it's fine, notice you shudder as he gets to his feet with his dick like a peeled banana in front of him. And then he jumps up on the sofa with one foot on either side of you. The rancid smell makes you woozy, you're about to retch but then you part your lips and let him into your mouth. You place a hand on each of his hairy buttocks and help him jerk back and forth. After a while he pulls out with a roar. You squeeze your eyes shut and close your mouth, dreading it, but enjoying it too, the warm spatter on your face. And when he's finally finished and you risk opening your eyes again, he's taken a hold around your dick, and then he opens his mouth and you suddenly can't hold anything back.

You waste no time in getting dressed afterwards, you're not able to stay there a moment longer, don't reply to Zombie, who's still sitting naked on the sofa, when he asks what the matter is, and leave, without a word, even though you were supposed to stay the night.

You're back the next weekend, and no sooner have you locked the door and drawn the curtains than your clothes are in a pile on the floor and Zombie is on you like a leech, and this time you moan out loud, can't be bothered trying to hide how good it feels, how much you've been looking forward to it, and then it's your turn, you can hardly wait, you grope frantically, a trembling passing through you as you get your hand around him, bend down, feel out of control and know you're going to come if you hear so much as a whimper from above.

Yet now and again you fall asleep on the mattress on the floor with a lump in your throat. You find the ever more imaginative nature of the fantasies acted out wildly arousing while they last, and extremely sad and shameful as soon as they're over. Everything is filthy, disgraceful and vulgar, nothing is natural or joyful. You look for signs of the same disgust in Zombie but he seems unaffected, as though he has no desire for anything more, as if he can't imagine there being something more. He seems satisfied. As though this is what he wants. As though this is the life he wants to live. You tell yourself over and over again that this time is the last, that you're not going back anymore, that you're finished with that filth, once and for all. And a week later you're back, your stomach bubbling with excitement and an erection so hard it feels like your dick could come into contact with the ceiling.

At school you act like you don't know one another, don't look at each other and ensure you always keep your distance. The thought of it being found out, what the two of you are up to, if the rumor was to get out, fills you with terror. And those times that, without wanting to and sometimes in the middle of class, you suddenly picture Zombie straddling you, a listless look in his eyes like a huge elephant, or the two of you spooning in bed and groaning loudly, it's like a nightmare from someone else's brain infringing on your own, a crazy image from someone else's life which just for a moment gets sent on the wrong frequency.

Bente's room is in the basement. You envy her that little den, it's almost like she has an entire floor to herself, secluded from the day-to-day on the upper floor, where it feels like your room has walls of glass. You sneak in there from time to time when you're alone in the house. After a while you always spend the hallowed hour, the one after school's finished, before anyone else is home, in there. You don't get up to much, just mooch around, sit in the wicker chair, lie down on her duvet, take a sniff at the creams and perfumes, the ones that almost make you puke if she gets too close, but which in there, free from her, smell lovely and excite you. You look through her drawers but never find anything worthwhile.

One day you ransack the wardrobes, and at the bottom of one, beneath a pile of clothes, you find some dirty panties. The smell is fantastic, you get an erection at once. You check the time, still a good while before they're home. Then you undress and pull on the panties carefully, the girlish wriggles you have to perform in order to fit into them making you numb with randiness. You try to tuck your dick down into them but it's so hard it feels like it'll snap. You're trembling as you walk over to the mirror and almost pass out when you see yourself, your hairy thighs sticking out from the lace trim, the bulge around your veiny scrotum and your cock bursting out of everything so sweet and feminine.

You turn toward the bed and have hardly taken hold of your stiff member when heavy jets of sperm pump out over her flowery pillowcase.

You're walking home from Zombie's, the sun was shining while the day lasted but now it smells of winter again, the sky is dark blue, almost black, and down from the railway track a brittle membrane grows over everything that's got wet during the day. A girl comes out of the underpass by the kindergarten and you see who it is straightaway. You speed up a little and catch up with her at the first speed bump.

"Hi!" you say loudly.

She goes over on her ankle, dropping her gym bag on the ground. There's a flash in her eyes as she turns and sees who it is.

"Where are you off to?" you ask, in the same loud voice, as if you're standing several meters apart. A newspaper sticks up from the melted ice on the asphalt between you, lying sodden and torn like an injured bird.

"Home," Unn says, but hesitates as though she's unsure she understood the question. Then she draws a breath and adopts what's probably supposed to be an untroubled air, just as hard-ass as she's been every time you've seen her since Easter, and bends down to pick up her bag. But fear is showing behind the aloof expression.

"And you?"

You don't answer, just stare at her with a look you hope she discerns some evil within.

She turns to go but you grab her arm and hold her back.

"What is it?" she asks.

"Come with me," you say.

"Where?"

"In there."

You nod in the direction of the kindergarten.

"Why?"

"I want to show you something."

"I need to get home."

She tries to pull away but you tighten your grip.

"I want to show you something."

"What?"

"Come," you say. She looks around, ready to scream. But there isn't another living soul in sight. Calm and purposeful, you take her the entire way around the playground and over behind the long main building. You shove her down the steps in front of you to the storage cellar, and without letting go of the sleeve of her jacket, you draw the knife from your pocket and prize loose the metal staple from the wall the padlock is hanging from. Unn asks what you're planning to do. You relish the fear in her voice, push her into the darkness and close the door behind you. It's as black as a grave. And while the two of you are standing opposite one another but unable to see one another, you can feel her anxiety, rising and rising, filling the whole room up like a tank of water.

"Aksel?"

Her voice is hoarse and frail.

"Aksel?"

Your hand is on the light switch, you can feel the smooth plastic beneath your fingertips, but you take your time before turning it on.

The glare from the light bulb in the ceiling is like a clap in what has been an interminable, undisturbed silence. Unn has her back to a shelf stacked with buckets of paint, both hands in front of her face. The concrete floor is sloped, streaks of dirt visible here and there, in one spot there's a few beer bottle caps lying next to a used condom and some soggy toilet paper.

"You've been going around telling people I raped you," you say.

She doesn't move, remains standing with her face hidden behind her hands. But a quick gleam from between her fingers is enough to let you know she's looking.

"So now I might as well do it. I mean, since you've already told everyone."

She takes her hands from her face, folding her arms across her chest instead. You go toward her. The box cutter as light as a little stick in your hand, her eyes fixed on it. You move right up close. The wrinkles around her eyes look like creases of dried glue. Then the tears come.

"Show me your cunt," you say.

Her whole body is shaking. But it doesn't seem like she heard what you said.

"Show me your cunt," you repeat, holding the knife up in front of her, level with her eyes.

She stares at you, as though wondering who you are. Then she loosens her buckle and begins to take off her jeans. You're wearing a pair of panties you've stolen from Bente, your dick swells, becoming hard and curved inside the smooth material. Unn is bent over struggling to take her jeans down. When they're around her ankles she straightens up and folds her arms again.

"All the way off," you say.

The tears plug up her throat like a cork, she sobs more than breathes, after a while she starts hiccupping.

"Get on with it."

She works her jeans and shoes off with her feet. You follow her clumsy, frantic movements closely, surprised you're not more worked up. But her fear has become your composure and the other way around. You're both in balance.

"And those," you say, pointing the blade of the knife at her crotch.

She hiccups loudly, and then burps; her mouth emits a smell, then a crackly noise, almost electrical-sounding, comes from between her teeth. She's comprised solely of complete terror. Yet still she waits a while before, without taking her eyes from you, she begins to jiggle off her panties. You glance down. Her pubic hair has a reddish tinge, and the skin looks like it's covered in black dots.

You retract the blade and bring the handle up between her legs, the opening for the knife against her genitals. Her face freezes. And then she starts to sing, a tremulous, high-pitched wailing coming from between her swollen lips, which resemble two dry mandarin wedges.

You stand like that for a long time. Neither of you know the outcome of what's been started. And the two of you remain standing in this uncertainty, motionless like a sculpture cast in the same mold.

Then, after a long time, you step back, put the knife in your pocket and wipe your hands together, as though you'd got some dirt on them.

"There," you say, your voice mild and friendly. "Now you can go."

She looks completely confused, her brain working overtime to figure out the information you've just given her.

"Weren't you on your way home?" you ask, smiling.

She takes a long time to understand that she's saved, that she can be on her way, without interference. And then there's a new flood of tears, proper crying this time, as though the plug in her throat has come loose and is being washed out. She picks up the gym bag, her clothes and shoes and walks toward the door, again making a noise as if singing. At the doorway she turns and looks at you, as though awaiting the final all clear. She looks like a refugee with all she owns in a bundle.

"Feel free to blab," you say. "Tell whoever you want."

She squints into the room. Her puffy face makes her appear Chinese.

"Nobody's going to believe you now anyway!"

Lunch break. The asphalt area like an exercise yard in a prison; the Tina Turner songs over the PA system sound like they're playing through a megaphone. You make sure to stay close to someone from the class, not too close, so they might take it upon themselves to talk to you, but not too far away either, so they don't get the impression you have nobody to talk to. You catch sight of Zombie, standing at the far end of the schoolyard, on his own by the bicycle racks. He doesn't even bother to pretend, to make out he's part of a group, just stands there, his arms hanging by his sides, waiting for time to pass.

Why does it have to be this way exactly? Why aren't there several worlds to choose between? Zombie turns his head now and again, observes the commotion around him, before resuming his statue-like vigil. Everyone can see it's quite unbearable for him to be there, but that he has to be, that he's confined to this, that there's nothing else, not for him, not for you, not for anyone.

You're sitting at the desk in your room, and in the window in front of you, beneath the triple blossom of the reading lamp, sits a consumptive scrag with dark rings under his eyes, looking at you. But the reflection at night is always like that: no matter what faces you make or what way you stare, you appear just as scared and just as sickly, like a ghastly portent of the end of your life. The music is pleasant and soothing, the hollow sound of the flute and Ozzy Osbourne's voice suspend time and make the night everlasting, the darkness spreading like a lake flowing over and slowly but surely drowning everything that lives.

My name it means nothing
My fortune is less
My future is shrouded in dark wilderness
Sunshine is far away, clouds linger on
Everything I possessed—Now they are gone
You look like an insect with the black headphones on. The transformation has begun, you think. By daybreak it'll be complete. The only thing they'll find tomorrow will be a horrible little beetle, hidden in some fluff and dust in a corner of your room. And you can picture your mother, standing there yelling at the terrified insect, demanding to know what on earth you have done, if you ever stop to consider anyone but yourself, how in heaven's name you could think of doing something like this, how could you think of doing it to her, and if you could only imagine what it's like for a mother when her son is changed into an insect, if you've so much as spared a thought as to what she's going to say to other people, when they see what's happened, if it's too much to ask if, just for once, someone in this house could have a little consideration for *her*?

Ingenuity knows no boundaries. Every time you meet you go a little further, become a little more uninhibited, show a little more barefaced enjoyment. Women's underwear becomes a regular feature. But even before you come, it's like you can sense that bad feeling that's on the way, the one which comes down like a cold hammer as soon as your sexual desire is satisfied. Every contemptible ejaculation moves you yet another step from how things would have been, how they should be, how you actually wish they were. Girls, parties, and good times, they all seem to belong to a distant galaxy. All things boyish and youthful fly right by. Nothing normal or joyous is within reach. It's like life itself is passing by overhead, while you're lying in a bra and lace panties down in Zombie's stinking basement sucking cock.

And in the desperate hours after yet another horrible orgasm you lie awake wishing everyone and everything would go to hell, fantasize for hours about how good things could have been if only they were different from how they are. You would have been able to put up with anything, anything at all, just not this. You would have got along with any people at all, just not those you're forced to fit in with. You would have coped with any "friends" at all, just not those "friends" you've been allocated. Suppose Oskar met with an accident and died, you think, then you'd never need to worry about anything. And you think about how meaningless it is that accidents occur so seldom, how such an unbelievable amount of people, considering how many people exist, *aren't* affected, in proportion to those who are. Oskar, who's even the kind of guy who likes taking chances, likes exposing himself to danger: why hasn't something ever happened to him, something that killed him or at the least injured him or disabled him for life? You can just see how amenable he'd become if he was sitting in a wheelchair. Or if he died, you swear to yourself that then, then, you would never complain about anything again, *then you would be one happy camper*, you would be immune to all forms of despair. And you can just see how well adjusted you'd be, if only Oskar didn't exist. You can see it so clearly, that if Oskar and Zombie were eliminated, how everything would open up for you, the stink would be expelled, fresh air would be let in, all your pain and sorrow driven out, *how life would be livable again*, how opportunities would present themselves, how all the good things in the world would be there to help yourself to. Such a glorious paradise the world would be, if only Oskar and Zombie weren't a part of it.

And they could take Uncle Syvert while they were at it, always asking you about stuff when the family are gathered, meaningless questions, like how old your teachers are and where they come from, which championships your school has won, that kind of thing, as if he has a sixth sense when it comes to sniffing out things you have no idea about, as if that's his greatest pleasure in life, to corner you.

And Rugstad, your math teacher, who's forever calling you up to the blackboard and always has an ironic quip ready for the class to enjoy. And Paulsen, the woodworking teacher, who leaves everyone to their own devices. And Amundsen, the PE teacher, who at the end of every session asks one of the best boys to decide what you're all going to play, which means floorball every fucking time. Actually they could take the whole class and swap it with a new one, there's no one you couldn't manage without, on the contrary, you wouldn't miss a single one of them, and you'd be sure to go on the offensive straight off with their replacements, so that none of them would have anything on you, anything they could conceivably use against you later.

Yes, they might as well take the whole lot, while they're at it, all your teachers, all your neighbors, all your relations, young and old, your entire family, each and every person you know or are connected to in any way, they could take them and get rid of them, no matter who took their place it would be for the better.

And so, in the darkness, on Zombie's stained spare mattress, you recreate the world as a good place to be, ruled with an iron fist, free of all those who prevent you living the life you want to live. And you imagine every single person you know, every single individual you know of, lined up on the edge of an enormous pit, and you walking along the grave with a gun in your hand shooting them in the head, one by one. And then afterwards you stand looking down, your whole life so far, your whole past up to this point, gathered together in a heap of torsos, arms and legs. And then a bulldozer would come along and fill it in, the grave closing on everything that up to now had been yours. And then you'd sit up in the colossus for the last time and drive back and forth across it and roll the ground flat, so in the end nobody could see there was a grave, all pressed down and smoothed over, as though nothing had ever taken place there, as though none of the people lying buried had ever walked the surface of the earth. And when you arrive home the replacements would be there. A new mother and a new father would be waiting with the dinner ready. A new sister would come up from the basement when called to come and eat. And at school the next day, there would be a new teacher to wish you all welcome. And when you took a look around the classroom all you'd see were new faces, with everyone's attractive, curious and slightly apprehensive features turned toward you with imploring looks, since you're the sole survivor of the last ones to have been there, consequently the only one who's familiar with the situation and knows how things are done. And they'd all come to you if there was something they were wondering about, even the teacher, since he didn't feel completely at home in his new role. And before too long they'd compete in order to have a few words with you when they see you have a moment to spare, they'd fight to win your favor, stand in line to make your acquaintance: you, the natural center of attention, the obvious leader.

But everything you thought would endure forever, everything you were sure only death alone could relieve, suddenly it's gone, suddenly nothing's left of it. In the course of a few dizzying days at Lillehammer High in the autumn of 1980 you realize that the nightmare is over. It's like crossing a threshold. Everything is new, fresh, and enticing. And for the first time in your life you experience an intense interest in the people around you, a profound, irresistible curiosity in other people, an urge to be with them, to take part in their lives, get an insight into their worlds, allow them to take part in yours, get to know you as a person, how you really are, all your secret dreams. For the first time you listen to your own needs and desires, for the first time you begin to carry them to fruition. Life abounds around you. Your every thought is coupled with joy. You're ready for whatever may come.

Never again will you have to adapt to please another person. Never again will you need to seek refuge in another place. Never again be disciplined. Never again lie down for someone. You're free. Zombie, Oskar, they're gone, the lot of them! Stein-Ove, Harald, Andreas. An entire society has ceased to exist. You've made a journey: all that's left of the old country is a distant memory. The move from one school to the other, the dissolution of the old class, the joyful farewell with classmates, the wonderful feeling of leaving them, of turning your back. And the fantastic discovery you made right away, that there's more people than the ones you've met till now, than the ones you've had to put up with till now. The fantastic discovery that conversations can be more than pretense, piss-taking, and intimidation. That there are people it's actually possible to like. And that you, Aksel Morander, are one of them, one of the people it's possible to like, one of them who's capable of liking others. You've been promoted. Promoted to humanity. You've become part of the society of the living. The love you feel merges with the love you evoke. You just hadn't realized: all you had to do was turn away, then you found yourself standing in the reality you'd been living in the shadow of. Now the shadow has receded, the colossus is gone, the road is clear and nothing is holding you back.

Oh, you were lost for so long! You were kept out of all this for so long. You've been asleep, you've been wandering in an endless night. You've been ignorant of everything. The magnesium of exiled yearning glows within you, seethes within you. Yes, the future you're suddenly faced with burns so brightly that you no longer see your gloomy past. Everything is yet to come, you think. *The darkness of my past is the light of my future.* And you realize, you understand, that this has been the intention all along. That what you thought would last your whole life, it was merely a prelude, an introduction. A new time awaited you. A new time, which is your reward for manifest perseverance. After the hells come the heavens. And you saw it through, you showed strength, you survived the ordeals and you were found worthy. What you thought was reality turned out to be the dream. Now, finally, you're awake.

That's when you see her. A girl you haven't noticed before. She's standing in the middle of a group, half a head shorter than the others: a chubby little face bordered by dark wavy hair. Now she's laughing at something someone's just said. And you see how she shines, like a cherry tree in bloom.

I can picture you, at the very moment you catch sight of her. Everyone around her disappears. And one single thought strikes you with sudden clarity, that if this laughter could one day be directed at you, then your happiness would be complete, then the world would be a place where you too could live.

And you feel a terrible joy pass through you, a terrible joy at being.

STIG SÆTERBAKKEN (1966–2012) was one of Norway's most acclaimed contemporary writers. His novels include *Through the Night*, *Self-Control*, *Siamese*, and *Invisible Hands* (all published by Dalkey Archive).

SEÁN KINSELLA holds an MPhil in literary translation from Trinity College, Dublin. He has previously translated work by Frode Grytten and Bjarte Breiteig into English.